OVER JORL

✥

OVER JORDAN

NORMA JOHNSTON

AN AVON CAMELOT BOOK

AVON BOOKS, INC.
1350 Avenue of the Americas
New York, New York 10019

Copyright © 1999 by Dryden Harris St. John, Inc.
Interior design by Kellan Peck
ISBN: 0-380-97635-8

Library of Congress Cataloging in Publication Data:

Johnston, Norma.
    Over Jordan / by Norma Johnston.
    p.   cm.
    Summary: In 1836, fourteen-year-old Roxana undertakes a dangerous journey up the
Ohio River to help her beloved servant, Joss, and Joss's fiance, a runaway slave, escape
to freedom, aided by Roxana's former teacher Harriet Beecher Stowe.
    1. Underground railroad—Juvenile fiction.   [1. Underground railroad—Fiction.   2. Slavery—
Fiction.   3. Afro-Americans—Fiction.]
    I. Title.
    PZ7.J64530v   1999   99-21938
    [Fic]—dc21   CIP
                                                                                                  AC

First Avon Camelot Printing: November 1999

CAMELOT TRADEMARK REG. U.S. PAT. OFF. AND IN OTHER COUNTRIES, MARCA REGISTRADA,
HECHO EN U.S.A.

Printed in the U.S.A.

FIRST EDITION

QPM   10   9   8   7   6   5   4   3   2   1

www.avonbooks.com

*Dedicated to the memory of
three valiant women:*

Harriet Tubman
Sojourner Truth
Harriet Beecher Stowe

OVER JORDAN

ONE

Joss was singing *Deep River* again.

She'd been singing that spiritual as long as Roxana could remember, ever since she'd come to Grey's Landing to be Roxana's nursery maid. That had been ten years ago, in 1826, when Roxana was only four and Joss was eight. Joss had arrived at twilight on one of the long Indiana summer evenings when Roxana had been wild to stay up chasing fireflies, and her nurse, old Mam Lucy, had been equally determined it was time for bed.

"I won't!" Roxana had shouted, and run into the house, bursting into Papa's study without knocking. Something in the air had checked Roxana's rush as soon as she'd entered. Papa and Mama were there, both looking solemn, and between them stood honey-skinned Joss, looking lost and scared. Then Joss's dark eyes had fallen on Roxana's tear-filled ones. Her face had softened, and for the first time Roxana had seen Joss's unforgettable smile.

"What you be crying about, young miss, in such a beautiful place as this?'' Joss had asked, as though gentling a young colt. Roxana had stopped in mid-howl, and Joss had held out her hand. "Why don't you tell Joss about it while I'm helping you get ready for bed? If that be all right with you, ma'am," she'd added quickly, turning to Mama.

Something tight inside Mama seemed to relax, and she'd nodded, and Joss had led Roxana off upstairs. That night was the first time Roxana heard Joss sing *Deep River*. From that moment she loved the song and she loved Joss, who over the years since had gone from being nursery maid to companion. *Almost a sister*, Roxana thought suddenly, and found herself breathless at the realization. Even in this northern state, for a young white lady to treat someone of another race as "family" would be shocking—and could bring shame, or worse, on Papa, even though Papa would have thoroughly understood. No one had ever told Roxana these things; she simply knew them.

And it's all so silly! Roxana thought indignantly. *As silly as it is that Papa can't say straight out how opposed he is to slavery! Why, slavery's been banned in Indiana, and Ohio, and—and the other states and territories north of the Ohio River for years now, even if it does still exist in Kentucky and Virginia and points south. Though parts of Kentucky, and Virginia where Aunt Darden lives, are further north than we are. It doesn't make sense!*

Come to think of it, a lot of the things Roxana had been hearing all her life no longer made sense. "Colored people"—that was the polite way of referring to other races—weren't supposed to be as smart as white folks, but Roxana knew better. Papa had been personally teaching Roxana, and Joss, too—though they weren't supposed to tell anybody that—for the past two years. *Joss learns some things faster, and better, than I do*, Roxana thought ruefully.

She twisted round in her rocker on the upper veranda to glance into the schoolroom where Joss was putting away the books assigned for their daily reading. *And as for color . . . why, her skin's not much darker than mine is. Especially when I forget a hat or parasol when going out in the midday sun, the way—*

Roxana slammed the door on memory that made painful tears spring to her eyes.

Don't think about that, she told herself, repeating the too familiar litany inside her head. *Think about something pleasant. If the pictures won't go away, pray them away, like Miss Hattie said. Or write them down.*

Except that lately the pictures wouldn't leave. Roxana wasn't sure anymore whether it was God who wouldn't let them go, or she herself. And she had already filled many copybooks with anguished words—

Don't think about that. Think about something pleasant. Roxana took a deep breath and wet her lips.

"Think about my birthday," she said, softly, to herself. "It's my fourteenth birthday, and Papa will be back from Louisville in time for early dinner. He's gone to fetch me something special, because fourteen's a special birthday, he's always said—"

She stopped abruptly. It hadn't been Papa who'd always said that; it had been Mama. Fourteen had been special to Mama because that was the age she'd been when she first met Papa. He and Uncle Owen, Mama's brother, had been twenty years old; students at William and Mary College in Virginia. That Easter, Uncle Owen had taken Papa home with him to Dardengrove, his family's plantation in Kentucky. They'd come riding across the spring-bright fields—racing, probably, Papa being Papa—and come upon Mama gathering herbs in the kitchen garden. The sunlight,

3

arrowing through the trees, had turned her wheat-colored hair to gold, Papa always said. The sight of her had made him jerk to a stop so fast he'd nearly fallen off his horse's back.

"I knew right then," Mama used to say, laughing, "that *this* was the man I was going to marry! No use saying fourteen was too young to know. I knew."

"Because I cut such a dashing figure with mud all across my boots and breeches," Papa'd say ruefully.

"Because you worried about your mount's well-being rather than worrying about your appearance," Mama would correct. Then her eyes would dance. "Your manly grace and dark eyes didn't hurt, of course."

Four years later, when Mama was eighteen, they had married. By then Papa was a new-minted lawyer. And, since his father had died of the swamp fever the year before, Papa was the proud owner of Grey's Landing, whose spreading acres his grandfather had staked out in Indiana Territory before there even was a United States of America. Papa was able to bring his bride across the river to a fine house of twelve rooms, plus outbuildings, barns, and cabins for the hands.

As a child Roxana had never tired of hearing the story of that arrival recited by old Mam Lucy. "Sun be just settin', an' de sky red, red—like a conjure-woman's firepot." The old woman's eyes would grow dreamy, and her voice, in the soft Gullah speech of her girlhood, would take on a magical singsong quality. "Up bluff from river we come, an' water she be like glass behind us. Afore us, pillars risin' up ter greet us, white white like ghosts against de darkness of de trees. Lights in all de windows—"

"Like now," small Roxana would interrupt, and Mam Lucy would flash her toothless grin.

4

"Yes, like now, dem lanterns. Only dat night be candles. I hear afterwards your papa, he done give a signal from de boat while we was mid-river, so de candles be lit in welcome. Up from de river we all come, us'n your papa's fieldhands—he didn't have as many den as now—carryin' your mama's trunks an' boxes, an' furniture what had been your great-gran'mama Darden's. An' when we reach de veranda, your papa, he scoop your mama up in his arms an' run wid her up de steps, across de veranda, through de doorway where Caesar was holding de door open, an' clear upstairs."

"And then what?" Roxana used to ask, wide-eyed.

"An' den ever'body went to bed," Mam Lucy would say with finality. "It be full dark by den, an' time for sleep." And she'd blow out the bedside candle and tuck Roxana in firmly for the night.

Mam Lucy, who'd been Mama's childhood nurse just as she'd become Roxana's, had been the only one of the Dardengrove slaves to come with Mama to Grey's Landing, though Grandfather Darden had offered to provide a full dozen prime field hands as part of Mama's dowry. Papa had pointed out courteously that slavery was banned in Indiana, and that anyway he didn't hold with people owning other people. And added that Grey's Landing was quite well staffed already, by hands who were given wages as well as food and housing, thank you very much. He'd known better than argue about Mam Lucy coming to Grey's Landing, though. "I tell him, I look after dat chile he marryin' since she nigh de size of a grasshopper, an' I ain't stoppin' now. An' if Indiana be a free state, den I be a free woman in Indiana an' kin live where I choose. An' I *choose* ter look after Miss Verena, an' dat jus' be dat!"

Mam Lucy was still looking after everyone, although by

now she was probably over eighty. Nobody knew for sure, because nobody kept track of slaves' ages, unless an overseer did, in the breeding books kept on plantation livestock. Mama hadn't known Mam Lucy's age, and Papa couldn't find out. The year after the wedding, Uncle Owen had inherited Dardengrove. When Roxana was four, Uncle Owen died, and after that nobody from Grey's Landing went to Dardengrove again. Uncle Owen's widow was a cold, beautiful woman about whom the less said the better.

. . . Why on earth, Roxana wondered, was she thinking of Aunt Darden after all these years? She couldn't even remember when they had last seen her, except that she somehow knew it had not been pleasant.

Pleasant. Think about something pleasant. Think about the present Papa had promised, because it was special to be fourteen. *Except that I'm not going to fall in love straight off*, Roxana thought. *Not likely! For one thing, there aren't any young men worth a patch of peas around here, and for another, Papa'd have the hide off them if they came near me! Not that I'd want them to. Every boy I've had anything to do with has been just plain silly. Except of course—* She stopped abruptly.

She'd been about to say *except George*, and it didn't pay to think about that.

Inside the house Joss's lovely contralto voice went on.

Deep River, Lord,
My home is over Jordan. . . .

The spiritual twisted cords of love and pain around Roxana's heart.

"I want to cross over into campground, Lord," sang Joss, setting the polished mahogany chairs in place around

6

the schoolroom table. She came out onto the upper veranda, smiling at Roxana. The lilt in Joss's voice meant she was thinking about Gideon Mapes, her beau. A "free black," as people of his race who'd never been slaves were called, he'd come to Indiana three years ago to work for the local blacksmith. Now he owned the smithy. He was tall and handsome, with one gold earring and a romantic scar across part of his dark face. He and Joss had been "walking out" together, mostly along the river, for about six months. But the memory that flashed, sharp and bright, behind Roxana's eyes was an image from an afternoon much earlier, soon after Joss had come.

"Is Joss a slave, Mama?" four-year-old Roxana had asked. A shadow, half sadness, half anger, had crossed Mama's face before she replied.

"She was, dear. But she's not anymore. Your papa doesn't believe in owning folks as slaves."

"Do *you*, Mama?" Roxana had asked, puzzled, and Mama answered, "I don't *now*. When I lived in Kentucky, before I married Papa, I didn't know any better." Seeing the puzzled look on Roxana's face, she'd sat down with her beneath the willows on the river bluff and explained what slavery was, and why it was so wrong. She also explained that *Deep River* didn't mean the Ohio, which flowed below the bluffs. To slaves who dreamed of release from bondage, *over Jordan* meant "out of slavery into freedom." It also meant "heaven."

"I'm glad Joss is over Jordan!" Roxana had cried out passionately, meaning that Joss was free and living at Grey's Landing. And Mama, eyes wet, had hugged Roxana and whispered, "So am I. I think she was meant to come here."

After that Roxana loved Joss only slightly less than she loved beautiful, laughing Mama, who'd passed on to her the gifts of art and music; almost as much as she loved quiet, deep-thinking Papa, who was now a judge and a behind-the-scenes figure in Indiana politics. She loved Joss, a little guiltily, a bit more than her own rambunctious brother George, who was born two years after her, in 1824. With Papa, with Mama, Roxana had explored every inch of Grey's Landing, more than a farm and less than a plantation. With Joss and with George, she'd explored further along the woodlands and the river shore than her parents, had they known, would have allowed.

Roxana had wept buckets when, the spring she was going on eleven, Papa decreed she must attend Miss Catherine Beecher's new Western Female Institute, upriver in Cincinnati, Ohio. At first Roxana had been miserably homesick. Then she had found a kindred soul—not another student, but her teacher, tiny Miss Hattie Beecher. Miss Hattie, too, was musical, and a fine artist, and her long-dead mother's name had been Roxana.

Then in an instant, in one whirl of weather and river, everything had changed. Mama and George, on their way to bring Roxana home for summer vacation, were drowned in a terrible riverboat accident. A grave, silent Papa had come to Cincinnati to take Roxana home, and there was no more Western Female Institute for her, no more formal schooling. That had been June 1834. It was June 1836 now. Mama's absence was still a cold ache within Roxana that would not go away. She could no longer bear to play music, and the river filled her heart with terror.

It still scared her, even when quiet as it was today, Roxana admitted, looking down on it from the upstairs porch Mama had called a gallery. She never told anyone, not Mam Lucy, not even Joss, that she still had nightmares about the accident. She felt sick to her stomach every time she knew

Papa had to go "on the river," even when it was just to cross over to the Louisville side. When he had to go by steamboat for a journey of some days, she lived in panic. When she gave him a good-bye hug each time he left Grey's Landing, and whispered "Stay safe," only God knew that she was really saying "Don't die." She thought it again now, as she watched the shadows deepen along the river shore. Papa had promised to come home early. Why wasn't he here?

"Young miss!" Joss's voice called in mock sternness. "You aiming to have your papa find you traipsing round with mud on your skirts and stockings, after him ordering up a fine dinner for your birthday? You old enough to enjoy the judge telling your Aunt Darden you the lady of the house, and he can't spare you to go to that Young Ladies' Seminary she was so hellbent on recommending you for, you old enough to stop messing with weeds and mudpies."

"She's not my aunt, she's my mother's brother's widow," Roxana retorted. "And the reason she was hell-bent on meddling in my education, after years of us not having sight nor sound of her, wasn't because of her sudden sense of duty to her dear, dead sister-in-law's child—" She stopped, swallowed, and went on. "It was because she knew it would rile the living daylights out of Papa. Which it did, thank goodness." She swallowed again. *Drat*, she thought violently. Just when she'd started being able to mention Mama without breaking—

"I know, sugar, I know." Joss gave her a hug and then a slight swat. "All the same, you're a mess head to foot, and the judge due any minute. No time to heat water for a bath, so you'll have to do the best you can with bowl and pitcher. I declare," she added, steering Roxana towards her bedroom, "I don't know which of you has a more irresistible attraction to mud, you or that dog of yours."

"I wasn't messing in the mud," Roxana said with dignity. "I was gathering herbs to try making some more fomentations out of Mama's herbal receipt book. In case your Gideon needs something to draw the poison out of his hand again. 'A well brought up lady has to know how to heal the persons of her household,' " she added, imitating Mam Lucy's words and tone. She shot a sideways look at Joss, and giggled. "I'll admit Gideon Mapes isn't a member of our household—yet."

Joss didn't rise to the bait. She unhooked the back of Roxana's dress, pulled it down so Roxana could step out of it, and chuckled. "You sure landed in the mud, whether you intended to or not. Thanks to Golden Lad, no doubt? I saw him go galloping into the cookhouse, mud from chin to toes, and I heard Mam Lucy screeching for somebody to drag him out because she was just taking your birthday cake out of the oven! Mister Caesar gave him a bath under the kitchen pump."

"Poor Caesar," Roxana murmured guiltily. If she hadn't encouraged Golden Lad's wallowing in the mud, she hadn't stopped him, either. Caesar, butler at Grey's Landing since Great-Grandfather's day, was, like Mam Lucy, too old for the work each insisted on still doing.

She scrubbed herself, hard, with lavender-scented soap and rinsed off with the tepid water Joss poured from the washstand pitcher into the flowered bowl. "Help me do something with my hair, will you, please?" she asked Joss meekly.

"Mmm-*hmm*," Joss said with meaning, reaching for the hairbrush. "You go out in the midday sun without a hat or bonnet, you'll raise a crop of freckles. Not to mention your hair getting bleached like straw.''

"Don't start. I know yellow hair's not fashionable, but it's what I inherited. I'll try to remember to put a hat on next time." Roxana wrapped herself in the towel Joss handed her and crossed to gaze anxiously into the bureau mirror. Joss was right. Her nose and cheekbones did show a slight sunburn, and her hair looked awful.

"Don't worry, we'll see you don't shock your papa. Just you dress quick," Joss said dryly, holding ready a clean top petticoat and the pale blue muslin that was Roxana's best party dress. "You better tell the judge to give you a present of money for some new dress lengths," she commented, hooking Roxana up. "You grow another inch and this dress will be indecent. It's more than four inches above your ankles already." Four inches above the ankle was the maximum a young lady could show and still remain a lady.

"I can't help it if I'm growing fast." Roxana winced as Joss went to work on her tangled curls. "Papa's already planned something special for my birthday gift. That's why he went to Louisville today. Anyway, he'd never think of yard goods."

"Then you remind him. Unless you want Mrs. Darden writing to lecture him on your wardrobe as well as your education." Joss spoke lightly, but her voice had a twist in it that made Roxana look up in surprise. But Joss's face, reflected in the mirror, was averted. She finished tying a blue hairbow at the nape of Roxana's neck, and crossed the room to stow the discarded garments in the hamper.

Faintly, from outside the long open windows, came a toot.

"That's Papa coming!" Roxana bolted onto the gallery. The sky was a deep lilac now, and the air was fragrant with the scent of climbing roses. The small local ferry had pulled to a stop at the landing that gave her house its name, and Papa was galloping up the steep path to the bluff.

"*Papa!*" Roxana shouted and waved her arms. Then she gathered up her skirts and ran into the house and down the stairs. From somewhere behind them, Golden Lad came charging, shaking off droplets of water. They reached the steps of the veranda just in time for Roxana to run down into her father's arms.

"Whoa! Is this the greeting a young lady gives to a respected judge?" Judge Grey asked teasingly. But his eyes, she noticed with a shock as he released her, were like steel.

TWO

Golden Lad was pushing his favorite ball into the judge's pocket. Instead of responding as expected, the judge just patted the dog's head and kept walking toward the steps.

"Papa, what's wrong?" Roxana asked apprehensively.

"Now why should anything be wrong? I'm just reeling from the realization my daughter's nearly a young lady," he answered lightly. "I hadn't realized how you've shot up," he went on, echoing Joss's words as they went up the steps arm in arm. "I'll have to bring you back a trunk of goods for some new frocks."

"Bring *back?* Papa—"

"Never mind. I'll explain that later. Mam Lucy has the birthday feast ready, doesn't she? We mustn't keep her waiting." He hurried her into the dining room, all pale green and white. The mahogany table was decked with garden roses. Candle flames flickered above tall silver candlesticks, sending rainbow shafts dancing from cut crystal. Mam Lucy and Caesar were doing the birthday feast up proud. *As though I were a grown lady presiding at a grand collation, instead of having dinner with Papa, just the two of us,* Roxana thought. Suddenly, with a sharpness like physical pain, she wished her mother were there.

She sat on the chair Papa was holding for her, and unfolded her napkin with fingers that were trembling.

A small pile of packages waited at her place. A flat box whose formal wrapping bore signs of having come from Aunt Darden; friendlier packages from Mam Lucy, Caesar, and Joss. Caesar was standing properly behind Papa's chair, but his eyes were as eager as those of Mam Lucy, who, with the privilege of years of service, hovered with Joss in the doorway. Roxana, who knew the routine, opened Mam Lucy's package first. It contained, as she'd known it would, lace-edged linens for her hope chest, exquisitely embroidered with a wreath of Roxana's favorite flowers and her monogram, *RDG*. Mam Lucy was making sure Roxana would be provided for as Mama had been. Caesar's gift was a small wood replica of Golden Lad that he'd carved himself. Joss's gift was a crocheted reticule.

Roxana looked at her father, her eyes dancing. "Where's the gift you had to go clear to Louisville to fetch, Father dear?"

"That can wait till later. I can see Mam Lucy's anxious that her fine dinner doesn't get cold," the judge said, smiling at the old woman as she and Caesar started for the butler's pantry. Joss slipped out also; she always ate with Caesar and Mam Lucy, later, in the kitchen.

"On a night this hot, cold food would be a blessing," Roxana murmured wryly after they were gone.

As if in answer, the white muslin curtains billowed slightly. A faint breeze had sprung up, sending a rippling undercurrent through the room. Roxana shivered slightly.

The pale blue muslin, clinging damply to her shoulder blades, felt almost cold.

The birthday feast proceeded—melon from the garden, chicken with oranges and pecans, green beans and Mam Lucy's famous pilaf, cinnamon rolls—at a pace somehow faster than usual. The cake was produced; its candles blown out by Roxana in a single long puff.

"Won't be too many more years you'll be able to do that," Judge Grey said ruefully. He brought out a small box, which he set beside Roxana's plate. Something in his manner made Roxana unwrap it more carefully than she had the others. She flashed her father a faint smile, feeling suddenly shy, and lifted the box lid, the layer of cotton wool—

Behind her she heard Mam Lucy's sudden sharp intake of breath. Roxana's own voice, when she spoke, was trembling.

"Mama's locket."

"She meant you to have it, once you were a young lady," her father said. "That's why I had to go to the bank vault in Louisville today. If it had been in the house before that, you and that dog would have sniffed it out."

For a moment Mama's lovely gentle presence was all around. Then it faded, and Roxana was left, shaken, with the golden oval in her fingers. Grandfather Darden had given the locket, a copy of one belonging to an English ancestor, to Mama when she was confirmed. Its satin-finished gold bore on its surface the raised symbols of the communion service—an Easter lily; a chalice or communion cup; a cross and bunch of grapes—each picked out in tiny diamonds or rubies.

Inside, Roxana knew, were miniatures of Papa and Mama, as they'd looked on their wedding day, painted on ivory. She'd teethed on that locket when she was a baby; the toothmarks were still visible on front and back.

"Joss can clasp it on for you later. I'm all thumbs with women's fripperies," the judge's voice said, warm and teasing.

Even as Roxana shook her head, Joss entered, with an expression on her face Roxana couldn't read. "I beg your pardon, Judge, I thought you were finished dining. Will you be at home this evening? Gideon Mapes wants to come speak with you—"

"No, I'm sorry." Papa, who was never rude, actually interrupted. "It will have to wait. I have to leave for Washington in an hour."

After a split second's silence, Roxana's and Joss's voices both came together. Joss's urgent, quick, "Please! Can't he see you first? It's important." And Roxana's, "In an *hour*— you're not taking the steamboat—*Papa, no!*"

"I have to, pet," Judge Grey said quietly. Ignoring the cake, he folded his napkin and rose. "Caesar, pack for me, will you? Enough for a month's stay, or longer." The old man disappeared. Judge Grey slid his arm around Roxana as she willed her stomach to stay calm. "Come to the office with me while I pack my papers. You too, please, Joss," he added as they started for the hall.

Grey's Landing was built in the Palladian style, with a central block and two "dependencies," or one-story buildings, each connected to the main house by a pillared gallery. One contained the kitchen, pantry, and Mam Lucy's quarters; the other held Judge Grey's law offices. He went there now and began jamming books into his traveling satchel.

"Why do you have to go by river?" Roxana demanded. "And at *night!* Wait till morning, when things will be different—"

"Because I must," Judge Grey repeated. "There's trouble brewing this summer, Roxana. I can almost smell it. And when I was in Louisville today, I overheard two gentlemen talking at the inn." His voice twisted with disgust on the word *gentlemen*. "Someone knowledgeable has to talk to southern moderates about the slavery issue before extremists cause irreparable damage."

"Someone like you."

Judge Grey nodded. "I have friends on both sides of the issue, and some undecided. And I hold no office dependent on patronage." His judgeship was a lifetime appointment, not subject to renewal or vote. "I need to be in Washington as soon as possible." He turned to Joss. "I'm afraid you'll have to be responsible for my daughter for a day or so, until Mrs. Wilkins can be sent for."

"Papa! Not *her!* You don't know—"

"Yes, I do," the Judge interrupted. "Mrs. Wilkins is old, half deaf, very old-fashioned, and doesn't understand you. But she's a respectable widow, and you can't stay here for more than a night without a chaperone. Even that—"

"Then take me with you!" The words spilled out of Roxana faster than she could think them through. "You've always promised me a trip to Washington. We don't *have* to go by river. We could take the stage to Cincinnati, and then the railroad—I'd love to ride the new railroad—"

"It's out of the question, Roxana," her father said firmly. "You don't know what the capital's like in summer. There's disease in the air—"

"Then *you* shouldn't—"

"—and I'm going to be traveling hither and yon, conferring with congressmen and senators at their homes." He sat down at his desk, pulled pen and paper towards him quickly, and began to write. "Joss, have Caesar send one of the hands to Mrs. Wilkins with this tomorrow." He finished the note, folded it, and began to melt sealing-wax over a candle flame. "I don't quite trust my impetuous daughter to speed it on its way."

"Yes, of course, sir. But please, won't you spare a minute or two for Gideon—" Joss flushed. "That is, Mr. Mapes's business won't take long."

"Even a minute's too long tonight. I'm sorry. Why don't you tell me what's so urgent?" The judge pressed his signet ring into the melted wax that sealed the letter shut, then put it to one side.

The color came and went in Joss's face again. She straightened and spoke quietly. "Mr. Mapes wants to ask you for my hand in marriage."

Roxana let out a gasp of delight. Her father looked at Joss quizzically. "You're a free woman, Joss. You may marry whomever you choose."

"I live in your home. I look after your daughter. Mr. Mapes wants to do the honorable thing and ask you properly. He has money put by, and owns his own business—"

"Joss, Joss! I'll be glad to hear his character and financial references after I return. Of course you may marry him, if that's what you want. He seems a fine man, and has gained a good reputation in the three years he's been here."

Joss let her breath out in relief. "There's one other thing. We want to be married properly, not just jumping over the broom. I don't know if we'll be able to find a preacher willing to do the ceremony for us—"

"If you can't, I'll marry you two myself. I'm a judge for life, and don't have a congregation or constituency to worry about."

"Begging your pardon, sir, but you might be needed in Congress sometime soon," Joss said quietly.

18

"By the time I'm ready to give up a judgeship for the conflicts of Congress, pray God all that kind of prejudice will be worked out. If not, God help us." Judge Grey added a pile of papers from his desk drawer to the satchel, snapped it shut, and locked the drawer. "Go tell Caesar to send a hand to the blacksmith shop to say I can't see your Gideon Mapes tonight. Tomorrow you see him privately to explain why. And tell him I'd consider it a favor if he'd keep an eye on Grey's Landing while I'm gone. I'll trust you to take care of my daughter."

A look passed between them.

"Yes, sir. I'll keep the candles lit for you," Joss answered quietly.

She slipped out, a wraith in the gloaming that was closing in.

"What did that mean?" Roxana asked when she was gone.

"Sit down, Roxana." Judge Grey went to the door, looked out, then shut and locked it and closed the blinds at all the windows. "I did not want you to know about this until you were older. I was hoping you'd never have to know about it at all, but human nature being what it is, and the streak of self-interest, not to mention pigheaded blindness, that pervades this country—"

"*Papa!*"

"—but you shall have to do all the things your mother used to do for me in my absence." He came back to the desk and stood looking at her, his back against the bookshelves. "You heard what Joss said about keeping the candles lit for me. She meant the lanterns. They're signals, Roxana."

"Signals for what?"

"For runaway slaves. Most folks around here know I

don't hold with slavery. What they don't know is that for the past few years I, and a lot of other people—some friends, some I know by name, some not at all—have been acting as what you might call railway stations. Providing hiding places for slaves running away from brutal masters, or for those who are free but in danger of being dragged south and sold farther down the river."

The judge stopped, looking uncertain as to how—or whether—to go on. Roxana rushed in quickly.

"Where, Papa? And what do you do then? You mean you've had runaways hidden here, and I've never known?"

He gave a faint, humorless smile. "That was how it was meant to be. The more who know, the greater the danger."

To them, or to us? Roxana wondered. She jerked her attention back to her father's words.

". . . give them clothes and food and medical care. And when it's safe, smuggle them on to another stationmaster further north, till they're somewhere they can be really free and take new identities. That's why there are always lanterns in our windows. They're visible from the river, and from across the river in Kentucky. Because we have lights in all our river-side windows every night, the neighbors think nothing of them. But those who need them, know."

Roxana wet her lips. "How?"

"How did Joss know? I've never told her. She never gave a hint until tonight, but she just knew." Judge Grey paused. "Usually, when I'm going away, I put out the word to . . . our friends south of here . . . and an alternate station's used in my absence. Today I didn't have time to arrange for that. So I must trust you, Roxana, to be mistress of this station in my absence."

"And Joss," Roxana said shakily.

Her father shook his head faintly. "Joss must not be

perceived to be involved. I've heard of too many free Negroes being kidnapped and sold back into slavery by bounty
hunters." He unlocked a desk drawer and took out a
wooden box. "Here are the pistols you and Joss used when
I taught you target shooting. Take them to the main house
with you, and keep them loaded."

Roxana nodded, scarcely breathing. The drawer was
closed and relocked; another drawer was opened. "Here are
the account books for Grey's Landing. On the back pages
you'll find a list of all persons employed on Grey's Landing,
and their wages. The first of each month is payday. If I'm
not back by July first, you must pay the wages." Judge Grey
took a roll of bills from his waistcoat pocket, put it in the
drawer with the account books, and locked the drawer.
"I've brought enough money from the bank in town to
cover normal expenses for about six weeks."

He rose, pushed the heavy desk to one side, and kicked
back the Turkish rug. A trap door in the flooring lay ex-
posed. Roxana gasped, then caught herself quickly. Her father inserted a finger in a recessed brass ring and pulled the
trap door open. A set of narrow, steep stone steps led down
to darkness.

"They lead to a passage through the bluffs, ending in a
cave hidden by that tangle of briar bushes near the dock.
It's a way to and from the river. Do not ever allow it to
be used by daylight." He closed it, drew a ring of keys from
his pocket and locked it shut, covering it again with rug
and desk.

"Papa—"

"Don't interrupt. We haven't much more time. Do you
remember the old oven in the cellar fireplace? It used to
be part of the original winter kitchen." Roxana nodded.
"You'll find a loose brick in the fourth row from the bot-

21

tom. Come to think of it, you *did* find it when you were a child; that's how I discovered a good hiding place behind it. My strongbox is in there. Did you bring your mother's locket out here with you? Open it.''

She did so with trembling fingers.

"Look on the border of the frame around my picture. Take the magnifying glass.''

A string of numbers, separated by dashes, flashed up at her.

"The combination to the strongbox. First turn the dial right, then all around left to the second number, then right again. You understand. There's money in the box, a great deal of money, in case you need it. Also the documents proving Joss is not a slave. I anticipated there might be a time when they'd be needed closer than in the safe deposit box in Louisville,'' the judge added, to Roxana's shock. "The time could be coming. She knows where they are. You'll also find the list of other 'stations' there.''

He stopped, then sat down facing her, and took both her hands in his. "I've been saying fourteen is an important birthday, but I didn't know how important it might prove to be. You *will* have to be mistress of the house, and of the 'station,' in my absence, Roxana. That's one of the reasons I cannot take you with me when I've made no arrangements for a substitute. Caesar knows what's going on. Mam Lucy's doubtless guessed. However, you *must* keep the secret. Speak of it to no one except Caesar and Joss, and then only if some 'packages' come. That's the code word for travelers on the Underground Railway.''

Roxana started to smile, but stopped quickly at the expression in her father's eyes.

"I am deadly serious about this, Roxana. Being part of the Underground Railway is not safe for stationmasters, and even less safe for the travelers. People have been killed. The only way to be sure of not letting something slip to the wrong persons is not to speak of it at all."

"I understand, Papa," Roxana said soberly.

"In my absence, Grey's Landing and all who live and work here will be your responsibility—to look after, and to protect. That's a heavy load for anyone, let alone a young woman of fourteen. I must ask you to grow up very quickly, and for that I'm sorry." He placed the heavy key-ring in Roxana's hands and closed her fingers tight around it. "I needn't tell you, need I, to keep these safe? By the way, there are bullets in a bottom drawer. It wouldn't hurt for you and Joss to practice your target shooting. From what I've heard in Louisville, the border states are like a powder keg this summer."

A faint knock sounded at the office door. Roxana froze, and the judge became alert. Then Caesar's voice came softly.

"Steamboat comin', Judge. I got yer bags."

The judge rose, and Roxana did too, shakily. He hugged her, then held her off and looked at her squarely. "I rely on you, Roxana."

He snuffed out the candle and went to the door, then turned. "Will you walk with me to the river?"

Everything in Roxana's heart and stomach screamed; *No!* She fought the fear and nausea back, and nodded.

They left the office, which Judge Grey locked behind them. He handed Roxana the ring of keys. Arms around each other, they walked down the path to the landing, Caesar and one of the young hands following with the luggage. A low horn called, and a twinkle of lights came ever closer across the quiet water. The steamboat drew to a stop and

23

a deckhand slung a rope around the winch on the landing post.

"God bless you, love. I'll write." Judge Grey kissed her forehead, then hugged her.

Roxana threw her arms around him and, standing on tiptoe, held him tight. "Take care," she whispered vehemently, and the voice inside her head screamed, *Don't die! Not you, too—*

He pulled himself away, gave her one more reassuring smile, and strode on board. Caesar gestured and the young hand lifted the luggage over the narrow expanse of water between boat and landing; a deckhand took them. The steamboat pulled away into the darkness.

The last thing she could see distinctly on the boat was the stained poster next to the main door, illuminated by a hanging lantern.

WANTED—DEAD OR ALIVE!!!
Runaway Slaves . . .

THREE

Roxana couldn't sleep that night.

At two in the morning, waking from fleeting dreams that left her haunted with a memory of wind and water, she crept out of bed. Cautiously, so as not to wake Joss, who slept in the dressing room adjoining, she tiptoed to the long windows opening onto the gallery, and slipped outside.

Moonlight silvered the white climbing roses that gave off such poignant fragrance, and touched lightly on the quiet waters of the river. At least it was calm! And most of Papa's route to Washington lay overland—*didn't it?*

If only the schoolroom window stood open, she could enter from the gallery, light a candle there without it being noticed, and look at the route in the big atlas. But Caesar had, following his usual routine when Papa was away, locked all windows except in Roxana's bedroom before retiring. She dared not try to go to the schoolroom from the upstairs hall, because that door squeaked. One sound would bring Joss to hover, comfort, *probe*—Roxana had learned to hide her fears, which grew rather than diminished during the passing years.

One sound—

There was more than one sound beginning in the upstairs hall right now . . . the whimpers with which Golden Lad signaled he was lonesome. Those faint cries could accelerate rapidly into howling if ignored. Swiftly Roxana tiptoed back into her bedroom, across the flowered rug to the hall door, and opened it just wide enough for the dog to slip inside. His tail was wagging and he was brimming with wet kisses.

Fortunately, now that he'd gotten where he wanted, he didn't bark. Roxana slid back into bed and he jumped up beside her. Cuddling with a large dog was not the most pleasant thing in the world on a hot night, but his presence was comforting. All the same, as the hours ticked by to morning, Roxana slept little.

"What ailed you last night?" Joss demanded, arriving with a breakfast tray, which she set on the table by the window. "And don't say 'nothing.' Your eyes look like two burned-out holes in a blanket."

Roxana didn't answer, and Joss's voice gentled. "It's the river again, isn't it? You've been dreaming of it again—or afeared of dreaming. Girl, when are you going to learn that fears not faced down keep getting worse?"

"I don't want to talk about it," Roxana mumbled, her face hidden in her nightgown. She pulled on a clean shift, and her dressing gown, and went to the table, not looking in Joss's direction.

"You better talk about it. If not to me or your papa or Mam Lucy, then to the doctor or the preacher. Even to that dog!" Joss added, glancing with meaning at the golden hairs on the sheets. "You got to get it out of your head, and into words, or those fears'll keep growing and growing, like the bogeymen in Mam Lucy's stories."

"I don't believe in bogeymen," Roxana said loftily, "and neither do you."

"No," Joss said gravely. "But I do believe in evil. And I know that fear can be one of the biggest instruments of evil. I do know that."

There was something in her tone that made Roxana look at her quickly. But this time it was Joss who turned away.

"Anyway," she said lightly, "you're worrying your head for nothing, because your papa told me he *is* making 'most all of his journey overland. So stop looking for trouble."

Caesar sent Willy, the ten-year-old son of Grey's Landing's washerwoman, over to the Widow Wilkins's house with the judge's letter. He returned, bringing the still sealed letter with him. "Miz Wilkins' gone to stay a spell with her married daughter upriver on the Wabash, where it's cooler. Least dat's what her field hands tol' me."

"Did you say why you was lookin' for her?" Caesar asked severely.

"Course not, a 'cause I don' know, do I? An' I brung de letter back 'cause I couldn't put it in her hand like you done said to," Willy said virtuously.

"You did just right," Roxana said quickly. "Go tell Mam Lucy to give you some of her blueberry muffins."

But when Mam Lucy herself appeared, she, Caesar, Joss, and Roxana looked at one another uneasily. "What we goin' ter do, young miss?" Mam Lucy asked, rubbing her hands on her long apron.

It was the first time she'd ever turned to Roxana with such a question, and the fact emphasized for Roxana both her altered status as mistress and the precarious nature of the situation.

"Nothing," she said. "Papa doesn't want anyone to know he took off for Washington so fast, so we do nothing. What we *don't* do is let it get out that I'm here without him or Mrs. Wilkins. For a lot of reasons."

She saw confirmation in the others' eyes. "Ain't proper you be here unchaperoned," Mam Lucy said reluctantly.

Roxana snorted.

It wasn't, after all, as though anyone would know. The farms along this stretch of the Ohio River were relatively isolated, and in summer's heat no one would think it strange that neither Roxana nor her father rode into town. Even church attendance dropped. The only visiting that took place in July or August was when relatives from farther south, or from large cities, came to stay a spell.

It's not likely Aunt Darden will descend, Roxana thought with relief, *and anyway she's not blood kin. I don't have any close blood kin but Papa.* The thought, for the first time in her life, made her feel lonely.

You'll just have to marry someone with lots of brothers and sisters and aunts and uncles and cousins, Mama had said once, *because neither Papa nor I can provide you with that. I only had your Uncle Owen, and he's gone.*

I have you and Papa and Georgie, Roxana had answered passionately. *And that's plenty!* Mama had laughed, and hugged her, and said she was glad Roxana felt that way for now, but that she'd feel differently once she was old enough for beaux.

That was when she told Roxana about the specialness of being fourteen.

. . . Why was she thinking of Mama so constantly, Roxana wondered with a start. Was it just because now she *was* fourteen? She fingered the locket uneasily.

A week went by. A letter arrived from Judge Grey, en route to Washington, saying he was fine and was traveling *overland*—he underlined the word. He would write again when he reached the capital, he said. Postage, Roxana knew, was far too expensive for letter writing to be indulged in often.

She began keeping a diary-letter that would either await his return or be sent to Washington, depending on his length of absence.

July brought payday to Grey's Landing. Roxana wasn't sure how to handle that responsibility. Mam Lucy was the most approachable, but after thinking hard, Roxana went downstairs right after breakfast and sought out Caesar. As butler, he was the real manager of the house and outranked other employees. To her surprise she detected a look of relief in his usually impassive eyes.

"Yes, Miss Zan. Folks'll be right glad to hear you're looking after it. What your mama did, when Judge away, she went to office an' got everything sorted out ready. Den she have me ring de big bell. An' whenever anyone ask her to keep money safe, she give 'em a piece of paper what told about it."

Thus prepared, Roxana went to the office, locked herself in, and with the aid of the account book sorted the bills into envelopes marked with employees' names. *Caesar, Lucy, Joss* . . . right down to Willy and the coins he was paid for doing errands. She was embarrassed to discover names she'd never even known. That was disgraceful, considering that Grey's Landing didn't have so very many hands. *Mama would have known them all*, she thought.

She locked the account book and the rest of the money up again, and went to tell Caesar he could ring the bell.

The tones had barely stopped reverberating across the fields when a line formed outside the office door, in strict order of rank. Caesar came first, and after he'd put his packet carefully away in his waistcoat pocket, he bowed and thanked her, then went to stand outside the door and admit others in turn. Roxana worked hard to memorize the faces that went with the names she hadn't recognized. Joss, like Caesar, took her whole pay packet, but most of the others asked her to put away all or part of theirs. Roxana wrote out careful receipts, which she knew they couldn't read any more than she could read their faces as they thanked her with bows or curtsies.

By the time she was finished she felt exhausted and, in some weird way, confused. She took a deep breath and looked up to find Caesar waiting silently in the doorway.

"Is there anything else I should do?" she asked.

"No, Miss Zan, you did just fine. What I needs to know is, we be going to celebrate Independence Day same as usual?"

Of course . . . the Fourth of July was only three days away. "*Exactly* as usual," Roxana said firmly. "You see to it, will you, Caesar? And thank you for helping me so much this morning."

Caesar's face softened. "It was an honor an' a privilege, Miss Zan. An' everyone'll be right down glad 'bout the celebration."

The anniversary of America's Declaration of Independence was traditionally marked at Grey's Landing in the way that Mr. John Adams himself had called for: ". . . solemn acts of devotion to God Almighty . . . pomp and parade, shows, games, sports, guns, bells, bonfires and

illuminations from one end of this continent to the other."
Great-Grandfather Grey, a Quaker from Philadelphia, had
gone back to visit his family there in June of 1776, taking
his son, then thirteen, with him.

"My grandfather knew a declaration of the colonies' independence was coming, and wanted my father to be able
to say he'd been there when it happened," Judge Grey had
told Roxana. Grandfather's own account, written down in
a blank-book now reposing in the judge's Louisville bank
vault, told an exciting tale. He'd seen Benjamin Franklin;
gotten to speak once to red-haired Thomas Jefferson, who
was drafting most of the Declaration; heard the rantings
and ravings of conflict coming through the open windows
of Independence Hall in the sweltering heat. Great-Grandfather and Grandfather had actually been in the street outside when news of the Declaration's passing had come, and
bells began to ring.

That had been sixty years ago, and in each of those
years the farm bell at Grey's Landing had been rung at the
exact time when the approval of the Declaration had been
announced. This year, in Judge Grey's absence, Roxana rang
it. She felt solemn and immeasurably old as she did so, and
then read the Declaration of Independence aloud to the
assembled house and field hands. But the solemnity wore
off as games and horseplay began. Aside from necessary
food preparation and care of animals, the day was always a
holiday for Grey's Landing people, and they made the most
of it. The celebration culminated in a picnic for everyone
on the bluffs, where they could watch the "bonfires and
illuminations" going on along, across, and on the Ohio
River.

Usually Judge Grey lit their bonfire. Tonight, at Roxana's request, Caesar did so. She wasn't afraid of fire, at least

not much, but with all those pitch-daubed knots of wood in the pile there was real chance of casualty if an amateur was involved. The flames leaped high, illumining Caesar's old, familiar features . . . Mam Lucy's, inscrutable; young Willy's, excited; Joss and her Gideon Mapes, more wrapped in each other than in the celebration; the field hands, their faces dark and unreadable.

"Thank you for inviting Gideon Mapes," Joss said much later, when she was helping Roxana get ready for bed.

"He's your fiancé. Of course he was welcome. Though I wonder whether either of you noticed much of the illuminations," Roxana added slyly. "It was splendid, all the lights and banners on the riverboats, and the torches on the docks along the river. There must have been bonfires and illuminations for miles inland on the Louisville side."

"They may not have all been for independence," Joss said quietly. And when Roxana asked what she meant, Joss did not answer.

The next day Caesar came home from market with news of rioting and burning in Kentucky, the result of bounty hunters coming through looking for runaway slaves. A steamboat taking cargo downriver to the slave auctions had hit a snag—a fallen tree in the river—and some slaves had escaped. Caesar told Mam Lucy, who told Joss, who told Roxana. Joss had never passed on such talk to her before. Roxana was conscious again that in some subtle way everyone's attitude toward her had altered. Because the judge was away, and she was in charge? Because she was now fourteen? *I suppose you have to be grown up at fourteen if you're a slave*, she thought, and was startled to realize the thought had never occurred to her before.

The fires in Kentucky burned again that night, and there were spurts of light showing along the shore and on the river. But no frightened "packages" followed the lanterns' beams to Grey's Landing in search of shelter.

The days passed quietly, with the hum of bees and the bright darting of butterflies in the garden. The mallard ducklings that had hatched in spring by the pond out back were almost as large now as their parents, and were growing their adult feathers, but still acted silly. Golden Lad went swimming daily and came home covered with mud. Roxana and Joss kept on with the studies Judge Grey had set out for them—mostly because Joss insisted.

"You want the judge to come home and find you've slipped backward in your learning?" she asked severely.

"You can't slip back on something you've already learned," Roxana said loftily. "Anyway, it's summer!"

"So your brains are taking a vacation?" Joss inquired. "Mmm-*hmm!*"

Roxana didn't answer. Instead of studying she spent mornings in the herb garden, often going there early, before breakfast, when the dew was still on leaves and flowers. Pale gray, blue green, green . . . yellow and white and blue. The lavender flowered, and the rose-lavender of chives; the silvery hoarhounds, rosemary, and wormwoods waved lacy fronds. *"Rosemary, that's for remembrance,"* she could almost hear her mother's loved voice quoting, and for the first time the sense of her mother's presence brought not an aching sadness but a kind of peace. *I am growing up*, she thought.

She gathered the herbs, washed them in rainwater from the barrel by the barn, and hung them to dry in the barn's latticed shade. In the afternoons she studied Mama's herbals, and receipt books, which often drove her in bewilderment to the judge's Latin dictionary. "So I'm really studying, after all," she thought.

The troubles across the river, so far as she could find out, had died down. No fleeing slaves came to the house by day or night. No neighbors called, so Roxana's being unchaperoned escaped notice. Gideon Mapes was occupied at his blacksmith shop all day, but after his supper, and on Sunday afternoons, he dressed himself in fawn-colored pantaloons, buff waistcoat and dark blue coat, and came courting Joss.

"Jus' like a white man," Mam Lucy muttered. It was impossible for Roxana to tell whether she was referring to his clothes or his behavior; whether she approved or disapproved. But, without having been told of Joss's betrothal, Mam Lucy began hemming and marking linens for Joss. It occurred to Roxana with a slight jolt that she didn't know what Joss's last name—if she had one—was. None of the Negroes she knew were called by last names, except for Gideon Mapes. Joss had always simply been Joss. The thought of asking Joss directly made Roxana turn red with embarrassment, and she was unable to get a glimpse of what second initial, if any, Mam Lucy was putting on those sheets and cases.

Another letter came from Judge Grey, en route to Washington. It made no reference to those strange, unsettling conversations on her birthday.

At the end of the second week of July, the unnatural calm was broken by a storm that set windowpanes rattling and churned the river's muddy waters. Lightning flashed, making Golden Lad point his nose to the heavens and howl. The rooster crowed at midnight, and several chickens panicked. One was caught by a fox; nothing was left in the morning but a pile of feathers. The thunderstorm stopped by morning, but for two days the skies were sullen, with intermittent showers and the atmosphere a strange yellow-gray.

"It doesn't even cool things off any," Roxana grumbled.

Joss didn't answer. For the two days of rainstorm Gideon Mapes had not come over, and she was oddly nervous.

"You know he still loves you," Roxana teased, but Joss did not pick up the bait. She just stared toward the river, in the direction of the blacksmith shop, her face unreadable. When Roxana waked in the night, the room was alive with shadows cast by scudding clouds. A breeze lifted the curtains by the open windows, and she could make out Joss's figure pacing on the gallery that faced the river.

The sun shone brightly the next day, and the air was full of an oppressive heat. Even the bees, circling in the phlox, were drowsy. Curtains hung limply. When Golden Lad bounced in, happily covered with green slime from the pond, Roxana herself dragged him out to the pump and washed him. The cool water from underground felt good. Something in the air, she thought, is infecting our mood the way the summer cholera Miss Hattie talked about infected citizens in Cincinnati.

She didn't mention this to Joss, or to Mam Lucy, because she knew what their reactions would be. Joss would snort and tell her she was getting fanciful again. Mam Lucy's eyes would go opaque. Mam Lucy knew far more than she ever let on, and sometimes thinking about that made Roxana shiver.

There were fires over on the Louisville shore again that night. And in the morning, Sunday, the air was again filled with a yellow-gray haze. Mam Lucy looked at the sky and squinted.

"Storm comin'," she murmured. Whether she meant that literally or not was impossible to tell.

Ordinarily on Sundays the Greys drove into town to church, and sat in the judge's customary pew, third row back from the pulpit. House servants, and any farmhands who wished to come, followed in the wagon and sat in the upstairs balcony. Now, with Judge Grey away, Roxana stayed home, for her presence without a chaperone would have caused comment.

The hours dragged, for few activities were allowed on Sunday. No needlework or gardening, for those were labor. No games, for they were frivolous amusement. No books except religious ones, preferably the Bible. When they were little, Roxana and George used to stretch out on their stomachs while she read Bible stories aloud, puzzling out the difficult words. They particularly liked the exciting ones about Moses and the plagues, Joshua and the Battle of Jericho, David and Goliath. Today, Roxana was too restless for reading, and anyway, Bible stories still brought heartache.

She was swaying back and forth on the porch swing when Caesar approached in the late afternoon, looking worried.

"Miz Roxana, you seen young Willie round hereabouts lately?"

"No." Roxana frowned, caught by his manner. "Is something wrong?"

"Nobody seen him for the past two hours. It's 'most his suppertime, and his mam's dat worried." Caesar nodded slightly over his shoulder, and there was Elvira, the Grey's Landing washerwoman, twisting her Sunday apron anxiously.

Elvira never came into the house except to deliver the piles of fragrant, starched ironing.

"He's probably down by the river and lost track of time. You go back to your cabin and don't worry." Roxana jumped up, grateful for something to do. "I'm sure I can find him." Down by the river fishing, she thought, amused. She and her brother George had not been the only children at Grey's Landing who chafed at Sabbath-day restrictions.

She walked sedately until she was round the corner of the house and out of Caesar's view. Then she picked up her skirts and sprinted for the paddocks. A lost child, certainly, justified a gallop on a Sunday afternoon!

Papa's Jupiter was grazing quietly in his favorite paddock. Roxana whistled and he came loping, hoping for carrots or a sugar lump. "Shh, Jupiter," Roxana whispered, glancing warily about before slipping between the crossbars of the fence. Then she stepped up on the lower bar, kilted up her skirts, and whistled again.

Jupiter lined himself up beside her, pressing close, and waiting. It was an old conspiracy they'd often acted out. He held himself motionless as she grabbed his mane and swung herself up bareback. Papa would have had ten fits, but Papa wasn't there to see as she rode Jupiter once round the paddock, then backed off and raced forward, clearing the fence in a beautiful leap.

It wouldn't hurt to take one good ride round a few acres before heading for the obvious fishing place by the river.

She was cantering happily through the pine grove when she heard a sound that sent a shiver through her. A child's voice, screaming—

Not waiting for command, Jupiter took off towards the river. Roxana dug her fingers into his mane and hung on for dear life.

It was only minutes before they cleared the trees and were on the open flat beside the river, where a large man was twisting Willie's arm.

"*Willie!*" Roxana shouted.

The boy stopped struggling briefly—just long enough for the man to lock him in a grip of iron—and screamed, "MIZ ROXANA!"

Roxana and Jupiter charged. Jupiter stopped short, but not before knocking the man backward slightly. In that moment, Willie jerked free. The man swore violently, and a knife flashed.

"*Don't make a move towards my boy Willie!*" Roxana shouted. She drew herself up as tall as she could, her eyes flashing.

"*Your* boy?"

"Mine, sir! I am the daughter of Judge Grey of Grey's Landing, and this boy serves me!" *Please, God, don't let him see I'm scared*, she prayed silently. "How dare you lay a hand on him!"

To her astonishment and relief, her words took effect. The man backed away slightly, wiping his hands on his breeches and pulling off his hat. "Your knife, too," Roxana ordered icily. The knife was put away, but one ham-like hand groped towards another pocket.

It came out holding a paper, not a revolver. "Begging your pardon, miss. I'm authorized to take custody of a darky of this description what's run away, and how was I to know?" The man unfolded the paper and held it out. It was stained, and reeked of stale tobacco. Roxana scanned it without touching it, and raised an eyebrow.

"You thought Willie was a youth of *fourteen?* Do you take me for a fool, or are you one yourself?" Roxana turned to Willie. "You get yourself home and be grateful if your mama doesn't whup you. And you, sir—" One signal of her fingers in Jupiter's mane, and Jupiter whirled and reared, knocking the man backwards. "While your chosen occupation may be legal, there is no room for it or you on Grey's

Landing acres. If you set foot here again, or raise a hand against one of our *darkies*"—she fairly spat the word—"be assured the judge will see that you regret it!"

She dug her heels into Jupiter's sides and galloped up the bluff, not slowing until she was out of the man's sight. Then she started to shake, not knowing whether to laugh or cry. The words she'd used! At last some of the ripe dialogue she'd read in forbidden novels had come in handy! But all the same—

She was able to breathe naturally by the time she cantered back to the house.

By then early dusk was falling, and Joss was so perturbed about Roxana's galloping bareback—"And on a *Sunday!*"—that she neglected to ask what had prompted the inappropriate behavior. Roxana, for reasons she didn't quite understand herself, didn't tell her about the confrontation.

On Sundays dinner was served at midday, after church, and the evening meal was what Mama had called "tea." Roxana cleaned herself up, and went downstairs, and ate, and kept her silence. She didn't say anything later either, when Joss tried to pry the explanation out of her while she undressed. "I have a headache," she told Joss evasively, and Joss said "Mmm-*hmm*," with meaning, but did not pry. It was not till Roxana was in bed, and alone, that she could let down her guard and start to shake.

She knew exactly what had happened, and what danger she had been in. *Slave catchers,* she thought. *Bounty hunters, looking for a reward like the one promised on that poster on the ferryboat.* The judge had explained about them, but the reality had never come home before.

Papa knew they were roundabout, she realized. *That's why he talked to me the way he did. That's why the lanterns.*

Thank God the lanterns had not, so far, been needed. . . .

She blew out her bedside candle and, somewhat to her own later surprise, she slept.

It seemed only moments later that Joss's hand was shaking her shoulder. Roxana blinked dazedly and looked up. The room was still in darkness except for moonlight. Joss's face was like a carved mask.

"Roxana, wake up. There's a package come."

"Package? Oh—!" Roxana sprang out of bed, trembling, and began to unbutton her nightgown. Joss stopped her.

"No time to dress. Put on your robe and come."

Silently, Roxana obeyed. Silently, she hurried down the stairs on Joss's heels. "Joss, where—?"

Joss put her finger to her lips and pointed to the study door. Roxana opened it and stepped inside, shakily, as a tall figure by the window finished closing the blinds and turned to face her in the darkness, a dim shape in the faint glow of Joss's candle.

Behind her, Joss shut the study door and touched the candle to a lamp. The room sprang to life, and Roxana choked back a gasp.

The tall, bronze man before her was Gideon Mapes.

FOUR

For a moment Roxana just stared. Then she turned to Joss in bewilderment. "Where—? You said there was a package—Why—?"

"I'm the package, Miss Roxana," Gideon Mapes said quietly.

"But you can't be—You're *free*—"

Her words sounded stupid, and her voice spiraled. She choked it off quickly. Joss was pushing a chair forward, saying urgently, "Zan, just *listen!*" Roxana sat obediently, staring at Gideon Mapes, at the taut muscle by his right temple that was twitching, at the almost unnoticeable scar that slashed across the left side of his face.

Joss went to stand beside him, linking her arm through his and pressing close. Her face was gray in the flickering lamplight, and her eyes were frightened.

"I emancipated myself, Miss Roxana," Gideon Mapes said. "I belonged to a plantation in Virginia, where I was taught the blacksmith trade. A few years ago, at a nearby plantation . . ." He hesitated, and Roxana saw Joss's hand tighten on his arm. "There was trouble—a man of my color by the name of Nat Turner started a slaves' rebellion. I took no part in the rebellion, though some others at our plantation did; I believed in the reasons but not the ways. . . . There were lynchings, torture, murders—of both blacks and whites. The owner of my plantation was killed, and his eldest wounded. I was lucky, I only got some burns and this—" He rubbed his hand across the scar. "I got away in the woods. I took myself to Cincinnati. There were many free people of color there, doing well, and I found work. But then the Registration was put in, and it wasn't safe there for me no more."

Roxana didn't know what Registration meant, but she could guess. "So you came here," she said, thinking out loud. "You're doing so well here. Everybody likes you. And you and Joss—What's happened? *Oh!*" Suddenly something clicked. "The bounty hunter."

"What do you know about bounty hunters?" Gideon Mapes asked sharply.

"One of them was on our land today, trying to drag off Willie." She heard Joss gasp. So for once the grapevine hadn't reached Joss's ears. Or perhaps Willie'd kept quiet about his adventure for fear of a licking. "Jupiter and I gave the man what-for, and he left."

"Are you *sure?*" Joss demanded.

Roxana stared back and began to shake. "I didn't stay to see," she said weakly.

"Word came to me of a bounty hunter at the tavern in town," Gideon Mapes said. "Asking about a 'nigger' of my description. I can't stay to find out if anyone knows. So I've come to you, Miss Roxana, which isn't right, seeing as the judge's not home. I know about the lanterns. Joss tells me you're tending them while Judge's away. Can you help me?"

"Of course!" Roxana spoke firmly, although the shaking was spreading inside. "My father left a list of stations. First thing in the morning—"

"He can't go back to the blacksmith shop," Joss cut in. "He's posted a notice saying he's gone away for a spell, and he's brought his clothes." She pointed to a carpenter's bag on the floor beside the table. "He'll have to stay here till you can get him off."

"Of course." Roxana thought rapidly. "He can sleep on the sofa in here. Caesar and Mam Lucy will have to know, but they're safe as houses."

Gideon looked at Joss, who nodded. Roxana rose. "I'll leave you in Joss's hands then. She'll fix a bed for you. Good night." She slipped out, and made her way upstairs in the darkness. It was not till she was back in bed that she realized she was still trembling.

It seemed like hours later that she heard Joss tiptoe into the dressing room, and the bed there creak, and then the sound of Joss's weeping.

In the morning everything was unnaturally ordinary. The shutters were closed at the study windows, but then they usually were in summer's heat. It was clear from the look in Caesar's eyes, and Mam Lucy's, that they knew, but they said nothing. After breakfast Roxana went with Joss to the study. Gideon Mapes was standing, hands behind his back, before a large map hanging on one wall. "Studying the routes to freedom," he said quietly.

"That's right, I don't know the route yet," Roxana exclaimed. She would have to look in the cellar strongbox, and didn't want to say so. To her surprise, Joss spoke.

"Caesar will know."

Why am I surprised? Roxana thought bemusedly. Caesar, when appealed to, had another and less pleasant surprise.

"Next station be ol' Miz Wilkins's. I druv de wagon dere often enough." He didn't add what they already knew, that Mrs. Wilkins was off at her married daughter's. "Nex' station be twenty mile further on upriver. " 'Sides, travel overland not safe wid dem bounty hunters near." He left as the other three turned to look at one another blankly.

"You'll have to hide here till they leave," Roxana said with more optimism than she felt.

That was Monday. On Tuesday it rained, and Willie, recovered from his scare, again went fishing, this time in the company of two slightly older Grey's Landing hands. They came back at suppertime, bringing ominous news. A whole posse of bounty hunters was rampaging from tavern to tavern, traveling secretly through the neighboring woods. Overland travel, they boasted, was "no longer safe for niggers." The information traveled to Caesar, to Mam Lucy, to Roxana—bypassing Joss, a sign of the household's respect for Roxana's new position, and its compassion for Joss. After dinner Roxana bolstered her courage and went to the study to break the news to Joss and Gideon.

"So you'll just have to stay here that much longer till they're gone," she finished.

Gideon Mapes shook his head. "Too dangerous for you, a young woman here with your father gone. I'll leave tonight."

"*We*," Joss corrected sharply. "I'm going with you."

"*No*, love—"

"Joss!"

Gideon and Roxana both spoke at once. Joss swung on

them, shaking with passion. "You think I'd let this good man go alone? Where he goes, I go. He *is* my life—"

"I won't let you," Gideon interrupted. "I'll go, and send for you when it's safe—"

"*No!*"

"*Wait a minute!*" Roxana shouted. "We're all being crazy! If you can't go by land, you'll have to go by water. On the riverboat to Cincinnati."

Cincinnati. The word hung in the air. *Of course*, Roxana thought. They would go to Cincinnati. To Miss Hattie. The Beechers hated slavery. Miss Hattie's father was the Reverend Lyman Beecher, the most famous preacher in America. The Beechers would know what to do.

For an instant Joss's eyes looked hopeful.

"You think a man of my color would be any safer on a riverboat?" Gideon Mapes asked bluntly. "With or without his woman?"

Roxana drove her fingernails into her palms. *God, show me what to do*, she prayed with all her strength. And as if in answer, she heard her own voice speaking.

"You would be if you were traveling with *me*. As my slaves."

The words seemed to come from nowhere. For a moment Roxana, thunderstruck, could scarcely realize that she'd said them. She dared not look at the others, for fear she'd offended them beyond all reason.

For several seconds silence hung in the air. Then Joss's arms were around her, holding her tight, almost rocking her before holding her off and questioning her with eyes afraid to hope. "Baby, the *river*?" Joss asked in a whisper.

Gideon, almost as quietly, said, "Begging your pardon, miss, but no one'd believe it, a miss young as you traveling alone with slaves."

"Yes, they would. If ah'm a southern young lady goin' no'th fo' th' summah to Cincinnati." Roxana's voice took on Aunt Darden's iron-willed southern butterfly tones. She didn't know where that voice had come from. But there was strength in it, strength that almost put starch in her own spine.

"Honey, are you sure?" Joss's eyes searched hers. Roxana just nodded.

"Where you going to get the fripperies to make you look like a woman grown?" Gideon Mapes asked skeptically.

"From the attic," Joss answered, looking at Roxana. "You're tall enough now."

Mama's clothes. Packed away so carefully by Mam Lucy, after—

She mustn't think about that. She mustn't lose her nerve. Roxana looked at Joss, at the unspoken question in Joss's eyes. "Yes, I can fit in Mama's clothes. Maybe even her shoes. I'll be . . . proud to go on the river with you."

And so they planned, late into that night and during the next day. They could not leave at once. First Gideon must grow enough beard to hide the recognizable scar. Word must be put out that Roxana had gone to meet her father. That was easily done; everyone in town would know that letters had come to her from Washington. It would be believed the judge had sent for her. And everyone roundabouts would take for granted that she'd traveled by carriage, then stagecoach, overland, because she was understandably afraid of water. Only Caesar and Mam Lucy would know the truth, and they'd tell no one.

It helped that the weather was so stifling hot that shutters had to be kept closed over all the open doors and

46

windows. Air came through the openings between their slats, but no real sun. More important, no one outside could see in. Mam Lucy, with Gideon Mapes's help, brought down the trunks of Mama's clothes, untouched these past two years. A faint fragrance of lavender, lemon balm, and verbena floated up as the lids were lifted.

"Look 'em over an' see what's easiest altered," Mam Lucy commanded. Roxana reached her hand out; drew it back as if stung, and turned away. It was Joss who lifted out the dresses and chemises, the nightgowns and wrappers and petticoats. They were as fresh as when they'd been laid away, needing only to be ironed—which was fortunate; had they been taken to the washhouse, Grey's Landing would have been abuzz with speculation.

With Mam Lucy supervising, Roxana tried on delicate lace-trimmed undergarments, let Joss lace her into a corset that nipped her waist until she thought she'd swoon. *If Mama could stand it, I can*, she told herself fiercely.

Joss dropped a flowered India muslin over Roxana's head. Mam Lucy sucked in her breath.

"I want to see, too," Roxana said loudly, and Joss cut in quickly, "No, wait." She untied Roxana's hair ribbon and twisted her hair up into a careless topknot.

Roxana turned to face the pier-glass mirror and stared. Mam Lucy and Joss were right, she *had* grown taller, enough so that Mama's hemline came on her to the currently fashionable ankle length. The pinned-up hair with side tendrils escaping into curls, the corseted waist and pushed-up bosom made her look—

"Like Mama," Roxana breathed involuntarily. And then, "But that's not good! So many people remember Mama—"

"No fear. We turn dat yellow hair fair wid walnut juice,

an' nobody know you," Mam Lucy said. *Fair* meant the much-admired pale brown that poets wrote about, considered much more beautiful than yellow. That afternoon Mam Lucy brewed up an evil-smelling concoction, and by next morning Roxana's hair was recognizable no more. In the meantime Joss had been mending or altering the summer garments that suited Roxana best. She should be, they decided, eighteen years of age. Old enough to travel, suitably guarded (that was how Gideon's presence would be explained) but not so old as to seem "worldly."

Roxana found a steamboat schedule in the judge's desk. A small packet-boat, the *Maria Q*, would come upriver in two days time, stopping at the nearest town, ten miles away, before heading north. "Best we travel after midnight. Most bounty hunters be sleeping off a drunk by then," Gideon said. They would go by one-horse chaise, light and quiet, through the deep woods, with the judge's Jupiter between the shafts. Jupiter knew every inch of the countryside for miles around, and was swift and silent. Moreover, he could find his way back home alone if so ordered.

The last day of waiting was nerve-wracking. Golden Lad, sensing a crisis, raced around and keened. He wanted Roxana to come out and run, but she dared not be seen with her altered hair. At last Caesar tied him up in the smokehouse.

The hours ticked by.

It was a heavy, sullen afternoon that threatened storm. *I won't think about it*, Roxana told herself fiercely. But she prayed a lot. She took her small prayer book and New Testament out of her trunk and tucked it in her reticule. Mam Lucy gave her dinner in the winter kitchen. The field hands had been told she'd already left to join her father, so no light must show through the dining-room shutters.

As the hall clock ticked away the evening hours, realization struck Roxana. This was the last time she'd wait here with Joss for anything. What would it be like here without Joss? Joss, who'd always been there, who'd mothered her after Mama died, who was going off into the good Lord alone knew what danger—

"Girl, you be sure 'bout dis?" Mam Lucy asked Joss suddenly, echoing Roxana's thoughts.

Joss, her eyes wet, nodded. "I can't *not* go," she said simply. "Gideon's my life."

She reached a hand for him but he, too, was aware of the gravity of the question. He drew away slightly. "Love, are you sure? It's not too late yet to change your mind, but it will be, soon. I can send for you later, when it's safer."

Joss shook her head hard. "It'll never be safe." She stopped, as if holding herself together, and then said suddenly, "Where's the broom?"

Everyone stared at her.

"I want to jump over the broom," Joss insisted. "It's the best we can do with the judge gone. I want to go with you as your wife, Gideon. Jumping over the broom may not be white folks' legal, but it's all our parents had, and *we'll* know we're bound."

Wordlessly Mam Lucy left the room, and Roxana followed. "What does she mean, 'jump over the broom'?" she demanded, as Mam Lucy rummaged in the butler's cupboard.

"Child, don' you know nothin'? Jumpin' over de broom be old African ritual for pledgin' marriage. All plantation owners allow, most times, an' take place often when dey *don'* allow it." Mam Lucy handed Roxana a broom. "Go dress dis up wid ribbons."

Roxana ran upstairs; came down again, having changed

into her blue muslin party dress and decked the broomhandle with her best ribbons and silk flowers. She also plucked the bouquet of lilies and roses out of the parlor vase, and carried it to Joss. They went into the parlor, where the shutters were closed tightly and the draperies drawn, where candles now blazed in silver candlesticks. No one seemed sure how to proceed. *I must stand in for Papa*, Roxana thought, and fetched her prayer book. She found the Ceremony for Solemnization of Marriage, and read the Scripture passages aloud. She passed the prayer book to Joss, and Joss read her vows, and Gideon repeated what she had said. Then Caesar laid the decorated broom before them and they joined hands and stepped over it together.

After that, more waiting. They reviewed their strategy for getting to the boat dock, then went over it again. They checked the luggage. Roxana mentally ran over her own responsibilities. *Dress*. It was too soon yet to put on Mama's clothes; besides, she'd avoid that corset as long as possible. *Golden Lad*. Tied outside, and sleeping. *Lanterns*. Unlit, for they daren't risk having anyone come tonight. Besides, she was supposed to be away, and the lanterns would not have been lit in the absence of all Greys. *Money—*

Roxana started. She must take money from Papa's strongbox, and this was something best done alone. She hurried to the pantry, lit one of the oil lamps Caesar kept lined up on a counter, and opened the narrow door tucked under the back stairs. A smell of damp earth sprang out at her. Steep, twisting steps led down into a yawning darkness. Her heart hammering, Roxana tucked up her skirts and began cautiously to pick her way down.

One step . . . another . . . be careful of the turn . . . At last her toes, inside their light slippers, felt the cellar's packed-earth floor. The old chimneypiece lay straight ahead, with its enormous hearth. The lamp flame flickered fitfully as Roxana felt her way. Here were the beginning of the hearthstones; here was the brick of the walls. A stale dust of ash assailed her lungs. Set the lamp down, carefully. Straighten, being careful not to bump her head. Feel for the edge of the chimneypiece, then bend again; feel for the oven built into the back wall. There it was, its iron door intact and its innards empty. Kneel down; move the lamp closer. Feel along the large, mold-covered bricks below the door. *Here* was the first row of bricks, the second, the third. *Here* was the fourth row. *Here* was the loose brick—

Roxana maneuvered it carefully, conscious of the passing of time and of the lamp that could be knocked over very easily. At last the brick was free. She inserted her right arm up to the elbow, and her fingers encountered metal . . . a handle-ring . . .

The box came out. *Quickly*, put back the brick. *Quickly*, creep backward, move the lamp further to one side, then stand. *Quickly*, with box under arm and lamp in hand, Roxana made her way across the cellar, to the stairs, then up. It seemed an eternity, rather than a minute, to reach the top. Then she was in the pantry, the lamp was on the counter, the cellar door was shut and locked. What now?

The box, emptied of valuables, could be hidden behind books in the library till she returned. No one touched those books except herself, Papa, and Caesar, who did the dusting and could be absolutely trusted. But it would be better to take the money out up in her bedroom, where no one could look through windows.

She ran upstairs.

Her bedroom was quiet, peaceful. A lamp burned on the bureau and another beside the bed, which had been turned down. The dress she would wear for traveling was hanging from the bedpost. Roxana set the strongbox on the bureau. The mirror gave back a reflection of herself covered with dirt and soot; her eyes looked like burnt-out holes. She would have to bathe. No time to think of that now. With shaky fingers Roxana unclasped her mother's locket; opened it and squinted at the numbers engraved, almost invisibly, around the frame. If only her fingers would behave! Remember Papa's instructions . . . turn the dial of the lock carefully: right, then left, then right again.

Three tries before, at last, she heard the lock click open. She lifted the box's lid.

Money. More than she had ever dreamed . . . bank notes overflowed the box, and beneath were gold coins. She couldn't leave these in the library; after removing what she guessed they'd need, she'd have to return the box to its hiding place, and lose valuable time.

She had no idea what would be needed. Perhaps she should take it all. The sewing bag that had been Mama's had a sturdy clasp. She emptied its contents into a bureau drawer; stuffed the bank notes and coins into the bag. Now what? Papa had said something about papers that would prove Joss's status. Roxana went rapidly through the box's remaining contents. Old business correspondence . . . letters between Papa and Mama when they were courting . . . a whole bundle marked *Emancipation Papers.*

Every person of color at Grey's Landing had once been a slave, she discovered with shock, hurrying through the papers with trembling fingers. Some of the papers were very old, dating back to Great-Grandfather Grey. In each case, slaves had been bought as the then master of Grey's Landing could afford them, and then set free, the purchase receipts pinned to the freedom papers. At last, at the bottom of the box, she found a fat sealed envelope marked *Joss Darden*.

Slaves, Roxana knew, sometimes took their owners' last names.

It was necessary to make sure the envelope did actually contain Joss's freedom papers. Roxana ripped it open.

There were the emancipation papers . . . no, it was Uncle Owen's will, open to its seventh page. Roxana gave it a curious glance, then froze as words leaped out at her.

> . . . *the negro wench Joss, which I begot upon the body of my slave Eliza in the year 1817, I bequeath to my sister Verena Grey, in the hope she will deal kindly with her.* . . .

The negro wench Joss, which I begot—

"So now you know," Joss's voice said quietly behind her.

Roxana whirled around.

Joss was standing in the doorway of the dressing room, a stack of folded clothing in her arms. Her loved familiar face was suddenly a stranger's, wary and on guard.

Roxana wet her lips. "You knew what was in the strongbox."

Joss nodded. "The judge showed me on my eighteenth birthday. He said I needed to know where to find the papers—and what was in them—in case anything ever happened while he was away." *Like now*, Roxana thought numbly. "Anyway, I already knew what they were. The emancipation papers your mama had the judge made out for me, so I'd be free, and the will that spelled out what I was and who I was to belong to once your uncle died. He left me to your mama so I'd be safe."

She said 'your uncle,' Roxana thought. *Not 'Colonel Darden.' Not 'my father.'* "I don't understand," she said stupidly.

"Yes, you do," Joss said in that same even voice. "You don't think I was the only half-breed at Dardengrove, do you?"

"Then how—" Roxana stopped. She meant how could Joss then have been a slave, and Joss knew it.

"One drop of nigger blood in you, an' you be nigger. I be half white, maybe more, make no difference." Joss never spoke like that, in the Gullah dialect Mam Lucy used, but she did so now, perhaps deliberately. "No difference to law, no difference to son an' heir of Dardengrove when it come to his own *git*. He want nigger bitch, so he took her, an' I be born slave."

Roxana flinched. A bitch was a female hunting dog, like Mr. Blessingham's Heart O' Gold, that was Golden Lad's mother. And Mama had long since instructed Roxana that the polite term for those of African descent, like Joss, was *colored*, or, more formally, *Negro*. She couldn't speak, and in the silence Joss's voice went on.

"You help us run, you need to understand *why* we run. Slave women cannot help themselves. White man own you, white man do what he want. Anyway, slave owners always want more slaves of good bloodlines, and what better bloodlines than their own?"

"But you're—" Roxana blurted, and then stopped. What should she say? *You're my mother's brother's daughter. You're my cousin. My Uncle Owen did this—* "You're my kin," she said at last.

Joss seemed to respond, without hearing, to Roxana's thoughts rather than to her words. "He left me to your blessed mother. So I'm free." Her voice petered out, like a music box run down.

"*Your* mother?" Roxana asked at last.

Joss became very busy putting garments into the hump-topped trunk. "Mrs. Darden sold her down the river soon as the colonel was in his grave. She couldn't sell me because of the will. That's why she hates your family so."

Roxana did the only thing she could. She went to Joss and wrapped her in her arms.

FIVE

Presently Joss straightened and wiped her eyes. "Enough of this. Time you get a bath and some sleep, dearie."

"You, too," Roxana said, for Joss looked exhausted.

The door opened and Mam Lucy entered, carrying steaming pails of water. "Off with you. I set up hip bath in guest room for you," she told Joss. "I'll tend to young miss."

"Where's Gideon?" Joss wanted to know.

"Gone to nap in library," Mam Lucy answered. "Fine man, he carry water up for me. Now hustle, girl. You be in need of sleep."

She shut the bedroom door behind Joss and turned back, her face inscrutable. *I wonder if she knows the truth about Joss*, Roxana thought. But of course she did. Mam Lucy—and Caesar too, no doubt—knew everything.

Roxana submitted to being washed and dried and tucked into bed by Mam Lucy. For once it was comforting to be treated like a child. One moment she was vaguely aware of Mam Lucy sitting beside her, singing softly. The next she was waking to the sound of Joss whispering, "Zan, wake up! Gideon says it's 'most time to leave!"

Roxana sat up, blinking. In the faint moonlight arrowing around the shutters she could make out Joss's form, oddly different somehow. Not till Joss lit the bureau lamp did she understand the reason. Joss was dressed, not in her usual pretty clothes, but in garments belonging to young Willie's mother, and her hair was covered with a kerchief. Roxana started to exclaim in protest and then, seeing Joss's eyes, bit back the words.

She slid out of bed and, with Joss's help, began her own transformation.

First the undergarments, and the dreaded corset. Then the full, ankle-length skirt of dove-colored muslin, trimmed with bands of dark blue satin ribbons. Next the tiny, pointed-waist bodice with dropped shoulderline and sleeves, narrow at the top, that widened before being drawn in at the wrist by more blue ribbon bands. The style had been so ahead of its time in 1834 that Mrs. Grey had never worn it, but it was just right for 1836. Made for traveling, it had another, low-cut bodice that could be worn for evening, and a jacket also. A triangular shawl, or fichu, of fine lace went round Roxana's shoulders, crisscrossed over the bosom, and tied at the waist in back. Roxana fastened it at the throat with her mother's brooch, the one containing braided twists of Darden grandparents' hair.

Joss surveyed her critically. "It will do," she decided. "Just so you remember to conduct yourself like a woman grown. Now sit so I can do your hair."

They were just finishing when Mam Lucy came in, carrying a straw bonnet that she had just retrimmed. "I allus did Miz Verena's hats," she said complacently, setting it over the high-piled braids Joss had arranged.

Roxana, starting at her reflection, almost gasped. Mam Lucy's eyes, too, had misted. "She sure does favor Miss Verena, she surely does," Joss whispered.

"She make her mama proud tonight," Mam Lucy said gruffly. "Now git movin'. Gideon Mapes say it be time you go."

He and Caesar were both waiting in the lower hall. "Your trunk's in the chaise, Miss Grey," Gideon Mapes said.

Miss Grey. Not "Miss Roxana." Title plus surname was what an eldest—or only—daughter was called on reaching young womanhood, while younger sisters remained forever with title plus first name. And Caesar copied this promotion to adulthood. "What you be callin' yourselves while travelin', Miss Grey? We best know so's we can tell de judge should he come home."

Names. Of course. They dared not travel under their own. Roxana found herself turning to Gideon instinctively. "Best to pick something that has the same initials, or has meaning for you, so you can remember," he said quietly. "I took Gideon 'cause I was partial to Gideon in the Bible."

"Then you could be George now," Roxana said. "For George Washington who freed this country." *And for my brother,* she added silently. "And Joss could be Jessie."

"What about you?" Joss asked.

Roxana's chin came up. "Darden! It's my middle name." Her mouth twisted. " 'Sides, it's a *southern* name, so I surely will remember to act like Aunt Darden about . . . everything. And 'Zan' stands for Alexandra, as well as Roxana. I shall be Miss Alexandra Darden." She went into the library, scribbled a few lines on a sheet of letter paper, folded and sealed it, and addressed it to her father in Washington. "I'll mail this from the next town we stop in upriver."

Upriver. It was time to face the river.

Roxana hugged Mam Lucy, whose lips moved in a soundless prayer. Caesar disappeared to lead Jupiter and the chaise along an almost invisible trail through the woods that would take them to the mouth of the underground tunnel. Roxana, Joss, and Gideon crept in total darkness through the portico and into the judge's office.

Shut the door tightly; lock it from inside. Make sure curtains are drawn and shutters shut. Light a single lantern. Fold back the rug. Unlock the trapdoor, turn it back, then down into darkness. Gideon held the lantern so Roxana and Joss could see to descend, then carefully arranged the rug so it would cover the trapdoor when closed from below. He handed the lantern down to Joss before climbing down himself.

The passage was narrow, hewn through earth and rock. It twisted, narrowing at times to almost crawl space. Roxana kilted up her skirt and prayed she wouldn't ruin her clothes. To arrive at the boat dock looking anything but proper would arouse suspicion. They groped their way in a downward path, Gideon leading, Joss bringing up the rear. The damp smell of earth and mold was permeated, ever more strongly, with a smell of tar and fish and dirty water.

The passage gave a final twist and ended in what looked to be a pile of stones but was actually primitive steps leading up into briar bushes, as Judge Grey had promised.

Gideon went up first, after handing the lantern to Roxana. He held the briar bushes aside for Joss to follow. Once up, Joss turned and knelt, reaching her hands back down for the lantern. Its flickering light illumined the bushes' crimson leaves, and Joss gave a laugh that was half a sob.

"They're burning bush. Let's hope the Lord's with us as He was with Moses." She passed the lantern to Gideon, who blew it out and pulled Roxana up.

They had emerged into a night silvered with stars. Not far distant the river lapped quietly. Hidden by trees, Jupiter waited like a statue between the chaise's shafts. Dark blankets and two hooded cloaks concealed Roxana's trunk. "Where are your trunks?" Roxana whispered.

Joss pointed to two small knapsacks. "Slaves travel light," she said flatly. She and Roxana put on the cloaks. Gideon handed them up into the chaise, then climbed up himself. Without a signal, Jupiter started off along the path. Caesar must have greased the axle, Roxana thought. There was not one squeak.

Then, as they circled back around the far reaches of Grey's Landing's fields, came another, too-familiar sound. Golden Lad, keening. The sound went on for several minutes before it died away.

They rode in silence for some time through the woods, near the river yet not so near as to be seen by passing boats. The chaise's wheels turned smoothly, and Jupiter's hoofs made no sound on the forest floor. Suddenly, Gideon jerked Jupiter to a stop.

"What—?" Roxana started, but his swift gesture silenced her. They crouched beneath the blankets, scarcely breathing.

Something was racing through the underbrush, as branches crackled noisily. *Something* was breathing heavily . . . banging against the light chaise . . . panting. . . .

Roxana jerked upright. Something large and gold and wiggling took a flying leap and landed in the chaise, covering her with kisses. Golden Lad, overcome with joy and pride—

Gideon gave a guttural exclamation, quickly stifled. Joss groaned. "We should have known he might break loose. Now what?"

"He'll have to come with us, there's no way round it." Roxana removed the leather belt that finished off her bodice, slipped it through the dog's collar, and anchored it tightly. The blue bowknot that decorated the buckle fluttered gaily. She threw the blanket over Golden Lad and planted her feet firmly on his back, and he settled quietly. Gideon grunted, and touched Jupiter's rump, and they moved on.

The sky was beginning to show streaks of light in the east. Presently Gideon began guiding Jupiter toward the right. "Where are we going? You're turning backward!" Roxana whispered in alarm.

"It be all right, Miz Darden," Gideon's voice answered soothingly. "We be headin' ter dock from northeast."

He had bypassed the riverport by circling it inland, so as to approach the dock from the opposite direction from Grey's Landing.

Miz Darden. Gideon's voice had coarsened, and shifted into dialect. It was time for the role-playing to begin.

Roxana and Joss sat up and shook out their clothes. They folded the cloaks and tucked them beneath the trunk straps. Golden Lad, too, shook himself and seated himself proudly at Roxana's side. As a rosy glow began to tint the treetops they swept down the dirt road from the bluff, a young southern gentlewoman with pet and slaves, bound for a cruise upriver.

Lights had not yet begun to go on in the windows of the houses, small in the distance, that they passed. The diagonal downhill journey ended where a few buildings backed, windowless, against the bluff and the road opened into a small open space. Before them lay a dock, a boathouse, and the river. Facing it, and now behind them, were a general store, a tavern, and a business office. Two backless benches ran parallel to the dock, and Jupiter came to a stop beside them.

Gideon climbed down and helped Roxana, and then Joss, down. He set the trunk and knapsacks by the benches. Golden Lad jumped out of his own accord, and curled up beside the trunk, eyes on Roxana. Gideon hesitated, looking at Jupiter, then he too turned to Roxana.

She went to Jupiter and stroked his silken muzzle. "Go home, boy. Go home!" she whispered. He licked her face, an old habit from her childhood. And then, obediently, he trotted off. Horse and chaise, quietly, moved up the road, up the bluff, growing smaller and smaller until they disappeared into the trees.

Roxana let her breath out and realized for the first time that she was trembling.

"Sit down, Miz Darden," Gideon said quietly.

She did so. "You'd better sit, too. We'll have to wait a spell," she said shakily. Joss smiled, but she and Gideon remained standing, side by side, faces wary and watchful.

Presently lights went on in the back of the tavern, and then in the front. Stevedores began appearing. A wagon clattered up, laden with goods to be shipped on the riverboat. There were covert glances in Roxana's direction, but no one approached them, no one spoke. Roxana had a curious sensation of seeing herself through Aunt Darden's eyes. *A young lady, traveling unchaperoned with dog and slaves? Appearing out of nowhere before dawn? Something wasn't right—*

She must not let herself think like that. She must be strong. Gideon's safety, and now Joss's, too, depended on her. She raised her head haughtily and stared toward the river, copying Aunt Darden's trick of not seeing what wasn't worth her notice. *God, don't let the river frighten me. . . .*

The riverboat was coming. Flurries of activity erupted around them, and from downriver came the unmistakable sound of the ship's bell and whistles. Golden Lad sat up straight, lifted his muzzle to the sky, and keened in concert. Roxana wound the "belt-leash" around her left hand swiftly and jerked it hard.

"*Down*, boy!" she ordered sharply. Golden Lad avoided her eyes but finally obeyed. Joss moved to stand behind Roxana. Her hand, unseen, took Roxana's right hand and squeezed it hard.

Roxana wanted to flash her a grateful glance, but caught herself in time. She shut her eyes and concentrated hard. *Remember, I'm a slave owner. Joss—no Jessie—is my slave. So is Gideon—George. He's here to wait on me—and guard me.* For that latter fact, at least, Roxana felt profoundly grateful. As to the rest—

For the first time it really struck Roxana how difficult this dangerous pretense could be. And how much worse it was for Joss and Gideon! They *knew* how it was to be slaves.

It was the first time that fact, too, had really struck Roxana, and the realization made her feel ashamed.

The bell and whistles grew louder. The steamboat was coming. The steamboat was here.

Roxana opened her eyes.

The morning sun was shining brightly now. It danced on the gilt paint adorning the upper railings of the boat now nosing to the pier. The lower deck was near invisible behind the cartons, stacks, and bales being shipped upriver. Roustabouts sprang forward to lash the boat to the iron rings of the pier. Other roustabouts piled on waiting cargo. A few passengers came ashore. Others, from the tavern and the waterfront, moved forward to go on board.

"Miz Darden, you want ah takes youah trunk on board now?" Gideon asked respectfully. His voice had lost all trace of education. Taking his cue, Roxana snapped her parasol open, lifted it, and rose. Golden Lad sprang up, his plumed tail waving madly. She jerked him back and he sat again, an injured expression in his eyes. A few spectators smiled or laughed. A well-dressed young man who had been leaning against the guardrail felt through his pockets and produced a cracker.

"May I?" he asked Roxana, nodding towards Golden Lad. Though his tone was properly formal, his eyes were dancing.

Golden Lad jumped to seize the cracker with enthusiasm. The young man chuckled, bowed politely, and strode away to become lost from sight in the crowd.

"Miz Darden, you best come now," Gideon's voice said warningly. He hoisted the trunk on his shoulder and led the way toward the gangplank. Roxana drew herself up tall and followed, and Joss fell in behind her.

A man in uniform jacket and cap demanded to see her tickets.

Roxana froze. So tickets ought be bought in advance . . . but from where? And for how much? Most of Papa's money was tucked securely inside her corset, inaccessible. Suppose she hadn't put enough in her purse? Joss's eyes, she saw, looked worried.

Roxana summoned up the memory of Aunt Darden's

voice and manner. "I have not had the opportunity to purchase them yet. I require accommodations for myself and servants to Cincinnati." She opened the chain-mesh purse hanging from her wrist.

The Darden manner must have worked. The man turned aside and conferred, returned to say, "You're in luck, young lady. Happens there's a fine cabin empty off the Ladies' Saloon." He named a price, which to her relief was within her purse's means. "Niggers can sleep on the deck below if they can find any space."

"My maid will sleep in my room, as always, in case I require her service in the night," Roxana said icily. *Dear detested Aunt Darden, who'd have known your hoity-toity airs would come in handy?* "And my father, Colonel Darden, insists that George guard my door when I travel." In a clan as large as the Dardens, there were bound to be lots of colonels. She just prayed the man wouldn't ask which one she meant.

The ruse worked. The man jerked his head, indicating that George should carry up the trunk, and selected a large iron key to hand Roxana. "Top of the stairs, turn right. So long's the wench knows her place she can stay with you. Your room's first off from the Main Saloon, so the black buck can stand guard over it from there, if nobody complains. They fix and eat their vittles on the lower deck where they belong."

Roxana was so angry that she dared not trust her voice. She swept past the man, nodding curtly for Gideon to follow. It was not until she felt a sudden lurch, and felt Golden Lad collide against her legs, yelping, that she realized she was indeed on a boat, and the boat was moving.

SIX

Joss's hand was at her elbow. Joss's voice hissed in Roxana's ear. "Don't look round. Just keep going. You can do it!"

Roxana closed her parasol and took a deep breath. "Come on, boy!" she ordered.

Propelled by Joss, pulled by Golden Lad who charged ahead, she went up the stairs. It helped that she had to hold tightly to the rail and to Golden Lad's lead. They followed in the wake of the very large Gideon, whose deep voice kept calling "Make way fo' Miz Darden . . . make way fo' mah mistress. . . ."

Roxana's heart pounded. People were staring, both at Gideon and at the bouncing dog. She dropped her eyes, taking refuge behind the brim of the stylish bonnet, watching her feet so she didn't trip on skirts unfamiliarly long. The carved railings surrounding the upper gallery were lined with shipboard spectators. From below came the shouts of roustabouts and the slosh of water. From overhead came the clang of the ship's bell and, again, that piercing whistle. Golden Lad planted himself and keened. The boat lurched, and a wave of panic washed over Roxana.

"Deep breaths!" Joss ordered, low, in her ear. Joss took the dog's leash from her fingers and steered her through the nearest doorway.

They were in a kind of drawing room ringed with doors, each one bearing a gaily painted picture. A group of men clustered around a bar, laughing and drinking, looked up as the little group passed. One man nudged another with his elbow, and both laughed. Golden Lad, of course, wanted to socialize. Roxana lifted her head higher and stared straight ahead. She heard Gideon's voice, humble and deferential, asking directions, and the careless answer, "Ladies' Saloon to the left, straight through them curtains, boy."

They passed between a pair of looped-back draperies, and were in another large room, also ringed with doors. There was flowered carpet on the floor, and settees, chairs and tables stood about. At the far end, instead of a bar, stood a bookcase. Some elderly ladies sat reading nearby. Joss took the key from Roxana's fingers, glanced at its number, and found the door. It was the first one beyond the draperies, and the name, above a picture of waterfalls, said *New York.*

It's named for a state. That must be why they're called staterooms, Roxana thought. It was a good omen. New York State, Gideon had said, was the best place for slaves to cross over into Canada and freedom.

Joss unlocked and opened the door. Gideon carried the trunk inside, set it down, and came back out. He and Joss exchanged glances and he jerked his head slightly towards the post where he would stand watching. "Heah yo' is, Miz

Alexandra," Joss said loudly for the benefit of listeners, and steered Roxana inside.

The stateroom was small and narrow, with a window at the end. A pair of beds—mattresses on shelves, really—rose along one side. Pegs for hanging dresses were affixed along the opposite wall. There was a tall chest of drawers, and a washstand with flowered bowl and pitcher. Beneath the window was a narrow dressing table and a backless stool, and beside it an armless rocking chair.

Roxana sat down on the lower bed, testing it gingerly. The mattress was straw, and lumpy. Golden Lad promptly jumped up beside her. Joss sat on the trunk, pulled off her headkerchief, and leaned forward to look Roxana squarely in the eyes. "You must not let yourself get in a panic again. And you mustn't let yourself get all riled up."

"I'm not riled up," Roxana said with dignity.

"Yes, you are. And I'm not speaking of these grand accommodations. You think I didn't hear that man's talking? Or the way he looked at me? Did I turn a hair?"

"He was so—awful. I don't know how you could stand it," Roxana said humbly.

"Folks like me are born knowing how. If not, they learn fast if they want to keep on living." Joss moved over to give Roxana a hug. "Child, I love you for hating people like that. But you'll have to be like them now, just a little bit, or you'll give us all away."

"I don't think I can."

"You have to just not notice things, and just not hear." Joss gave her another straight look. "You've been doing some of that all your life, or you wouldn't be so shocked now. You love Mam Lucy and Caesar, but how well do you really know them?"

Roxana turned her head away. Out the window, she

saw another boat pass by, its smokestacks awfully close. She shuddered. "I think I'll be seasick. Then there'll be no danger of my doing something wrong, because I'll be in here."

"No, you won't. The only way to make sure Gideon doesn't get sent down to that hellhole below for the whole trip is for you to be out and about and spitting fierce." Joss chuckled slightly. "Besides, I don't think a body can get seasick on a river as narrow as the Ohio."

She unlocked the trunk and began shaking out dresses and hanging them on the pegs. Outside the window, people promenaded along the gallery. Joss closed the shutters, leaving the slats open enough to let light in and let them see out, but not vice versa. Roxana stood up and smoothed her skirts. "I guess I'll go promenade, too," she said in a low voice.

"You do that. Find out where and when you're supposed to eat your dinner. I'll be here." Joss flashed Roxana a reassuring smile.

Golden Lad clearly intended to come along and that, too, was good. He dragged Roxana across the ladies' saloon to the nearest outer door. The smell of the river was stronger outside, but she scarcely noticed. She was too busy trying to make Golden Lad behave.

"Papa's right, he's spoiled," Roxana thought grimly, yanking him away from a spittoon. "I have to get him a proper leash. But where?" She had no idea how long it would be before the boat made its first stop. Or how long it would take to get to Cincinnati.

The boat suddenly lurched. Roxana went sprawling, and Golden Lad jerked free.

She grabbed for the nearest railing post, and felt a sudden pain shoot through her ankle. She sank back on her knees to reconnoiter. Then she was suddenly, humiliatingly aware that she was not alone. A pair of impeccable, costly boots stood before her, topped by equally impeccable fawn-colored trousers. A man's hand, elegantly gloved, was extended just within her line of vision. A voice said, "May I be of service?"

It was the young man from the pier. His voice was just as respectful, but his eyes were dancing. There was no help for it. Roxana put her hand in his, muttered "Thank you," and let him haul her up.

His amusement faded swiftly as he saw her wince. "You've hurt yourself, haven't you? Hold my arm, and let me seat you." He guided her to a rocker and she sank into it gratefully. "Shall I fetch that big darky of yours to carry you to your room?"

"No!" Roxana caught herself, remembering Joss's warning not to get riled by such words. "I would be much obliged, sir, if you would catch my dog for me."

"Most certainly. If the circumstances permit the presumption, may I introduce myself? Carlton Tanner, at your service." He bowed, then strode away, relieving her of the dilemma of whether to give her name. Mam Lucy, Roxana thought, would have approved.

He returned, leading Golden Lad by a length of rope. He also, despite what she had said, brought Gideon. "Now your own people can look after you. Pray do not hesitate to call upon me if I can be of further service, Miss Darden." Carlton Tanner tipped his fine beaver hat, bowed, and left.

So he had learned her name. "Not from me," Gideon said flatly, carrying Roxana to her stateroom. One other question was solved as he did so. A long table in the main saloon was being spread with a white cloth and set for midday dinner.

Joss, at Gideon's knock, opened the stateroom door cautiously. Then her eyes widened in alarm. "I'm all right," Roxana said quickly. "I just twisted my ankle and took a fall when that tarnation dog pulled free of me!"

They all looked at Golden Lad, now sitting in the center of the floor and grinning happily.

"I'd best take him down to Main Deck and give him walking lessons," Gideon said. "That's what they call the deck below, where the cargo and the boiler are. This fine deck, who knows why, is called the Boiler Deck." He turned to Joss. "Folks'll feel a heap sight more comfortable eating their dinner in the saloon if I'm not standing watching. Now she's twisted her ankle, Miss Zan's got a good excuse for keeping to her cabin. She'll be safe from unwanted attention. Not that all attention's necessarily unwanted," he added slyly.

Roxana blushed, and Joss looked at her with alarm. "It's nothing," Roxana said hastily. "And I'd be much obliged if—if George would give Golden Lad some training." Just in time she had remembered not to call him Mr. Mapes.

"Be happy to. The pup's a born searcher and retriever anyway." He picked up the rope, looked at it quizzically, and led Golden Lad to the door. "Don't worry, love," he told Joss gently. "I can learn things on the Main Deck, and I know my way around such places."

He means around such people, Roxana thought. She turned away so he could take his leave of Joss in private, and presently she heard the door shut and the key turn in the lock.

"Now, exactly what did he mean about *not* unwanted attention?" Joss demanded. Her words were different, but her tone was exactly what Mam Lucy would have used.

"It's nothing. When I lost my balance, Golden Lad got away. That young man who gave him a cracker on the

71

dock brought him back," Roxana said hastily. "His name's Carlton Tanner."

Joss's eyes filled with alarm. "You didn't give him your name!"

"Of course not!" Roxana didn't add that he had learned it all the same. "He was just being civil. He gave me his in case he could—" What was the term he had used? "Could be of further service."

"Mmm-*hmmm*."

"After all, he thought I was a woman grown."

"Just see's you behave like a *lady* grown," Joss warned. Her face was sober. "I never should have let you risk coming with us. I wouldn't have, except—" She stopped.

"Except you thought it was time I got over being scared. And you were right. Papa trusted me to look after the lanterns, to do the right thing. Well, coming upriver *was* the right thing. I'm still scared, but at least I got up the gumption. And if that means taking advantage of Mr. Tanner's offer of assistance, and acting 'least as old as you, and minding my tongue at the same time, then I'll do that too."

Roxana flounced, which was the wrong thing to do. Pain shot through her ankle.

"*Nothing*, hmm?" Joss knelt to strip off Roxana's neat kidskin traveling boot and her stocking. The ankle had ballooned enormously. "That settles it. No more peacocking on deck for a day or two at least, and it's probably just as well," Joss said firmly, filling the washbowl with water and setting it on the floor so Roxana could immerse her foot. Then she bound up the ankle and helped Roxana out of traveling clothes and corset and into a wrapper. "Stay on the bed and keep your foot up. I'll go fetch your dinner."

Joss returned, followed by a boat's waiter who carried a laden tray. "I can never—" Roxana started to exclaim, then stopped. Of course; the food would have to do for Joss too. And for Gideon, if they could get some to him. Folks who hadn't booked staterooms on the Boiler Deck— and certainly any people of color—had to bring their own victuals with them. That explained the greasy bundles she'd seen some bringing aboard, and the unpleasant food smells drifting up from below.

Joss and Roxana picnicked in the stateroom, then Joss packed some of the bread, cheese, and ham away and wrapped the rest to give to Gideon. "How?" Roxana asked. Neither Gideon nor Golden Lad had yet returned to the stateroom.

"Walk around the gallery till I see him below, and hand it down to him," Joss answered promptly, and left to do so. By the time she returned, leading Golden Lad, the afternoon light was beginning to pale. Roxana was startled to realize she'd been dozing.

"You've been asleep for a good two hours," Joss said. "You didn't get any sleep at all last night, and not much before that."

"Neither did you," Roxana said with compunction. "You get out of those clothes and lie down. I'll be able to go to dinner, and fetch some back for both of you."

"It's supper, and no, you won't. You best stay off that ankle at least another day. You want to scare the wits out of your Miss Harriet when we get to Cincinnati?" But Joss did take off her laborer's clothes and put on the pretty wrapper Roxana had given her last Christmas. She climbed into the upper berth, and Golden Lad jumped up beside Roxana and covered her with kisses.

"How did he act?" Roxana asked with apprehension.

Joss chuckled. "It's a good thing that dog can't talk. He's been socializing with folks of every race and station.

And that Mr. Tanner wanted to know how you're doing, and why the dog didn't have a proper leash. I told him," Joss said, shifting into an uneducated accent, " 'cause silly pup done chew it through on way to boat, sir, an' ain't been no time nohow ter replace it.' "

"You don't like him."

"Whether I like him's neither here nor there. What matters is what your papa and your blessed mother would think." Joss so seldom mentioned Mrs. Grey that Roxana started. "It's not right for him to be scraping acquaintance with a girl your age."

"Oh, pooh! I was lucky he was there, and anyway, he doesn't know my age."

"That," Joss retorted, "is my point exactly."

Roxana didn't answer, and soon she could tell from Joss's even breathing that she was asleep. She lay awake, scratching Golden Lad's silken ear and thinking hard. After a while a faint clatter of cutlery beyond the door told her the table was being set for supper. Roxana swung her legs over the side of the bunk, but the minute she tried to put her weight on her ankle she knew it wouldn't hold her. *Tarnation thunder!* she thought, borrowing her father's favorite exclamation. There being no help for it, she settled back on the bunk. Presently the sounds from beyond the stateroom door grew louder—ladies' voices and, from the Main Saloon beyond, male laughter and the clink of glasses. Golden Lad whined, and Joss sat up.

"I'll hand him back to Gideon, and fetch you some food, soon as I'm dressed."

"Fetch us *all* food."

"Mm-hmm. We'll be lucky if he doesn't help himself." Joss dressed quickly and picked up Golden Lad's rope lead. "Come along, you clown."

She was back in a remarkably short space of time, carrying a laden basket. "Mr. Tanner had it ordered and waiting. Mr. Tanner told me to be a good girl and take it straight to my mistress, and he'd take Boy down to the big nigger himself."

"I'm so sorry."

"No call for you to be sorry. He's from *Deep* South, can't you tell from his speech?" Joss didn't add the obvious; that the word 'nigger' was far from being used by slave owners only. "He must think Golden Lad's name is Boy because you call him by that so often."

They ate pickles and ham and biscuits in the stateroom as the sky beyond the shutters turned to gloaming. Joss tied the rest up in a napkin, dropped it in her pocket, and went to give it to Gideon. Left to herself, Roxana managed by hopping on one foot to get her nightclothes and undress. Back in the bunk, she undid her hair, brushed and braided it for the night, and at last lay down in the hot darkness. The dining sounds were over now, replaced at intervals by someone singing, and occasionally a whistle from a passing boat. It was—almost—possible to forget they were on the river.

Roxana folded her arms beneath the pillows and stared up at the underside of the berth above, wishing the heat would break. Tomorrow she'd have to do something about a leash for Golden Lad, but what? Was the next port on the Ohio or Kentucky side of the river? If she still couldn't stand, would it be safe for Gideon or Joss to go ashore alone and seek a shop? How many days would it take to reach Cincinnati? She hadn't thought to ask. . . .

She felt as though she were sinking deeper and deeper into a down comforter, except that the comforter was folded at the foot of the bed and not beneath her. No point in figuring that out, just snuggle in it. . . . The music was changing, becoming more like the rushing of the wind—no, the roar of water. The water roared and roiled, and the wind wailed and screamed, and everything was pitching violently, because waves were crashing over the boat, and they were sinking, going down and down, into dark waters and the endless screaming—

Roxana awoke abruptly, bolt upright in the bunk and shaking violently, soaking wet with sweat. The screams went on, and it was her own voice screaming.

"Shhh, shhh, child, it's all right." Joss's voice. It was *Joss* who held her, Joss who was smoothing back her hair and rocking her.

"I must have been dreaming—" Roxana swallowed hard and tried to breathe more slowly. Even with hands pressed hard together she couldn't stop the shaking or, to her shame, control her voice.

"I know, honey. It was the old nightmare, wasn't it?" Joss asked gently.

Roxana nodded.

Joss hugged her hard. "First time in more'n a year . . . I haven't seen you in a night terror this bad since two months after—" She stopped abruptly.

"You can say it," Roxana said steadily. "After Mama and George were drowned. No, I haven't . . . dreamt of it since then." She wouldn't frighten Joss by adding that the terrors in the months since had been in her thoughts, not in her dreams. "I'm sorry I scared you," she said humbly.

"Nothing to apologize for. 'Least not for you. I never should have let you set foot on water," Joss said grimly.

"You couldn't've stopped me. You're right; two years is time for me to face down my fears. Otherwise I'm not free either, am I? 'Cept nobody's told me how to control

76

my dreams. . . . Joss, I know it's awfully narrow, and too hot, but would you mind staying down in this bunk with me, just for tonight?"

" 'Course I will, honey." Joss slid in beside her and rocked her in her arms.

From somewhere beyond and below the stateroom window came, faintly, the sound of singing. Gideon's voice, deep and comforting.

"De-e-e-p river . . . my home is over Jordan. . . ."

SEVEN

"Why was Gideon down on the Main Deck for the night?" Roxana asked in the morning, and Joss replied that there had been complaints about his presence up where the "fine folks" stayed.

"I suppose someone didn't like his standing watch where he could see into the Ladies' Saloon. And that's all need be said about that," Joss said briefly. "You'd probably be scared of him there yourself, if you didn't know him."

Roxana winced. "He *is*—intimidating. So big and strong," she said carefully. "I guess that's to our advantage, isn't it? I mean, I feel much safer when he's near."

"I do, too," Joss said simply. "All the same . . ." She didn't finish. After several minutes she added briskly, "Anyway, down below he's able to lie down and get some sleep."

"On what?"

"Sacks of peanuts. They make real good bedding. I know, from when I belonged to Dardengrove."

"We're probably safer having him right below us," Roxana said, too brightly. "Why, if anyone tried to . . . be a nuisance to either of us . . . I just bet he could be up the deck post and on the gallery out there faster'n you could skin a possum!"

"A lot you know about skinning possum, young lady," Joss retorted. But she laughed.

Because of her ankle, Roxana stayed in the stateroom that day and the next. Joss left the stateroom to fetch Roxana's meals, and to see Gideon, and came back to report. Gideon took Golden Lad for walks on the Boiler Deck, and gave him lessons in deportment. Golden Lad spent the nights, happily exhausted, in the stateroom. When he appeared there for his third night on board, he was sporting a stylish bottle-green leather leash.

"Where did you get that?" Roxana demanded of Joss.

"I didn't. Gift of young Mr. God's Gift to Southern Ladies," Joss retorted. That was her private name for Carlton Tanner. "And well you might groan, missy. If we're not careful he'll be bird-dogging after us clear into Cincinnati. And that *could* be trouble. Folks there know who you are, remember. Whatever did you say or do to that young man to make him stick like glue?"

"I didn't say anything. But I'd better," Roxana said uneasily. The next day she hopped, with Joss's help, onto the gallery, where she settled into a rocker. Joss brought her dinner, then left her there with a book from the bookcase in the Ladies' Saloon, and Golden Lad at her side.

Golden Lad was an attention getter. Ladies strolling by stopped to admire him and to inquire about Roxana's ankle. Otherwise, she was left to herself, to read or think or watch the scenery unrolling like a scroll.

The Ohio River was narrow at this point, and the water quiet. Once or twice a steamboat passed, with an exchange of horns, bells, and whistles. More often they passed a flat-boat—large, carrying a huge load of logs, or small enough to hold only a one-room cabin, a small family, and a bit of cargo. Sometimes they passed a raft, poled by eager boys who eyed the steamboat enviously. One boy proudly held up a string of good-sized catfish, and the steamboat's horn tooted approval. Roxana laughed.

"Good afternoon, Miss Darden. I'm surely glad to see you're better."

Roxana jumped. There was no mistaking the voice, with its hint of a laugh, even before her eyes recognized the polished boots. She knew she was blushing, and longed fervently to keep looking down. But that was not what "Miss Darden" would do. She took a deep breath and lifted her head.

"Good afternoon, Mr. Tanner," she said.

He was leaning on the railing, a faint smile on his face, his hat in his gloved hand. An empty chair stood nearby. Roxana wondered whether politeness demanded, or forbade, her inviting him to sit. Playing the role of a young lady of marriageable age was harder than she'd expected. She looked away, and after a minute Carlton Tanner, in a different voice, said, "Pray forgive me. I did not mean to intrude. Look after your mistress, Boy."

Golden Lad's toenails scrabbled on the wooden flooring. The sound brought realization and a wave of shame. "It is I who've been rude, Mr. Tanner. Please forgive me." Roxana wet her lips and went on, avoiding his eyes. "I ought to have thanked you immediately for getting Boy a leash." She fumbled for her purse. "If you'll tell me what I owe you—"

"Please! Allow me the pleasure of making the leash a gift to your fine pup. It was no trouble, and a trifling sum."

He was making the leash a gift to Golden Lad, and not to her. That must prove he was a gentleman, one corner of Roxana's mind was thinking, just as another corner registered his further words. "—thought you'd rather trust me to select one than that hulking nigger of yours . . . Miss Darden? Are you all right?"

A voice she barely recognized as hers said coolly, "Of course. I am quite all right."

"No, you're not. You're white as a sheet." The other rocker creaked, which meant he had sat down. Roxana jerked her head away, breathing hard, gripping her chair seat in the effort to hold back the words rushing to her lips. *God, don't let me blow up at him*, she prayed silently. *It's too dangerous—*

The boat lurched sharply. Roxana couldn't help herself; she screamed. Not loudly, and quickly stifled, but Golden Lad keened in sympathy and Carlton Tanner bent toward her in concern.

"You *aren't* well. If there was real damage from that fall—you ought not to have attempted walking till you'd seen a doctor. Are you traveling far?"

"I *don't need* a doctor," Roxana muttered through gritted teeth. *What I need is to get rid of you*, she thought desperately. *And this tarnation corset. I can't even draw a proper breath—*

"Forgive me, but I think you do." Carlton Tanner pulled his chair closer and lowered his voice. "It's intolerable cheek of me to say this, I know, but I heard you cry out in pain last night. My cabin's the first off the Gents' Saloon, just beyond yours. I tried to inquire about you from that girl of yours, but she was very rude."

That voice Roxana scarcely recognized said, with silvery

precision, "I appreciate your concern, Mr. Tanner, but you are mistaken."

"I heard your voice coming from your stateroom. Crying out, just as you did now, but louder, longer. And then you spoke. I could not make out the words, but I recognized your voice," Carlton Tanner insisted. "I opened my door to see if help was needed, but by then the cries had stopped, and that nigra girl of yours was mumbling something soothing. So I decided I'd best pretend I'd never heard. But if your—" He floundered for words, because a gentleman could not mention *ankle*, or any other part of a lady's anatomy. "If you are still experiencing discomfort, it would be wise to leave the boat at the next town and seek a doctor, or have one summoned to the boat."

Roxana took a deep breath. How would Mama—or Miss Catherine Beecher, the much-feared headmistress of the Western Female Seminary—have answered? "I appreciate your delicacy, and your concern. But I have no need of medical assistance. The cries you've heard came not from pain, but from fear."

"Fear? Oh, you mean of those brutes down below—"

"*No*, sir! Of the river." Roxana shut her eyes for a moment, steeled herself, then took another breath. "I am very much afraid of—of maritime accidents. I dreamt of one last night. And just now, when the boat lurched—"

For a moment panic washed back over her, and she could scarcely breathe.

"Please excuse me. I really cannot talk of it." She put her hand out blindly toward the railing, and at once he jumped up and offered her his arm. "Allow me—"

"*No!* Please just—go." Roxana, teeth gritted, hauled herself to her feet and hobbled, using Golden Lad for support, back to her stateroom. Mercifully, Carlton Tanner did not follow.

Joss took one look at Roxana's face and hurried her inside. "Sweet Jesus, what happened?"

"Nothing! 'Least, nothing important, I don't think." Roxana sank with a gasp onto the lower bunk and submitted to having the boot pulled off, a painful process.

"Talk, girl," Joss ordered, hurrying for a basin of cold water. Golden Lad applied himself to massaging the ankle with his tongue.

"That's all right, it feels good," Roxana mumbled when Joss ordered him to stop. "I just made a fool of myself again. You were right, I've got to learn not to get riled up about—you know."

"Mmm-*hmm*. Mr. Carlton Tanner."

Roxana nodded. "Don't worry, I didn't say anything that puts you and Gideon Mapes in danger. He'd—heard me screech last night, and was sure either I or my ankle was in danger." She told the rest of the story quickly.

"Kind of man he is, he's not like to let it rest there." Joss frowned.

"He's not likely to want to speak to me after I was so rude. And *what* kind of man?"

"The kind that's taken a strong attraction to you from the moment he set eyes on you, is what. You'd best be prepared with a story that will make him lose interest in you *and* your nightmares," Joss warned.

Roxana groaned.

That night, well after Joss was asleep, Roxana lay awake. Actually, she was making herself stay awake for fear of further nightmares. She would nap during the daytime, she planned. She never seemed to have bad dreams then.

What would her father do if he were faced with a situation like this in a court of law? *You have to take the negatives and turn them to your advantage,* she'd heard him say. She remembered stories of how Great-Grandfather Grey, during the French and Indian Wars, had learned to anticipate an attack and strike first, gaining the advantage of surprise.

Carlton Tanner would certainly be surprised if she approached *him.* And maybe he'd be embarrassed.

She lay awake till nearly dawn, staring at the underside of the upper bunk and plotting. And when, at last, she slept for a while, she didn't dream.

Following Joss's orders, she kept her ankle elevated on a bolster, and by morning it had shrunk close to normal size. "Time you tested it out a bit," Joss declared, examining it after she'd brought breakfast. "*Mild* exercise. You want it to be stronger before we reach Cincinnati."

"Which will be when?" The main drawback to hiding out in the stateroom was that Roxana couldn't get any firsthand information.

"Another day or so. Depends on how much time it takes to pick up and unload cargo at how many stops— that's what Gideon hears. Seems this little boat doesn't bide by any particular schedule," Joss said with disapproval.

Joss was right, of course. A larger boat would have traveled faster and more dependably. But a larger boat might not have stopped near Grey's Landing for another day or so. And a larger boat, no matter how safe, would have *seemed* more scary.

"If you're bent on avoiding Mr. Carlton Tanner," Joss said, "you might consider reading for a spell in the Ladies' Saloon. It would give me a chance to give this stateroom a proper cleaning." Joss didn't think much of the efforts of the crew in that direction.

"I'll think about it," Roxana murmured. In mid-morning, using Golden Lad as a prop for her hobbling, she did take her book into the Ladies' Saloon. Golden Lad lay at her feet and basked in compliments from passing ladies. They expressed polite interest in her improving ankle, but did not intrude.

Roxana had picked up a copy of the *Best-Known Works of Wm. Shakespeare* and opened it at random to the second act of *Romeo and Juliet*. She'd read it while at Miss Beecher's school, and considered Romeo a show-off and Juliet a ninny. Now she was surprised to discover that she read with different eyes. Juliet, too, was fourteen and being forced to assume the manners and behavior of a lady. As for Romeo—

Why was she suddenly seeing Romeo with Carlton Tanner's face?

This won't do, she thought firmly, and turned to the next play in the collection. But that, too, had all too uncomfortable relevancy, for it was *Othello*, a tragedy of a dark-skinned African feared and mistrusted in a world of whites.

When the dinner gong rang Roxana retreated to the stateroom. Joss wouldn't urge her to eat in the Main Saloon, for having food brought to the stateroom was the only way to provide meals for Joss and Gideon. After Roxana ate, Joss wrapped the extra food and carried it down to the Main Deck beneath her apron. She ate down there with Gideon, and stayed as long as he thought was safe.

As soon as Joss left the stateroom, Roxana let down her hair, brushed it, and did it up again as best she could. It wasn't as good as Joss could have done, but Joss would emphatically have disapproved of her intentions. She couldn't change into an afternoon dress without Joss there to lace her up, so the muslin she'd worn that morning would have to do. The bonnet would cover deficiencies in hairdressing, and she knew the pale green muslin was becoming. She watched through the shutters until she saw Carlton Tanner go by, and then she and Golden Lad went out on deck.

Carlton Tanner was where Roxana expected, toward the bow, looking out upriver.

"Mr. Tanner," she said sweetly, "I've come to apologize."

She had the satisfaction of seeing him jump. He spun round, then hurried to find her a rocking chair. "There's no need—"

"Yes, there is. You expressed gentlemanly concern, and I behaved as though you'd been insufferably rude. My only excuse is that I was embarrassed. Please forgive me."

"There is nothing to forgive."

"You're very kind."

"But I can't help wondering—" He stopped. "Sorry. I'm being impertinent again."

Joss had been right, he wouldn't just drop it. Roxana took a deep breath. "You're wondering why, given my fear, I'm traveling on the river?"

"Guilty." He flashed a boyish grin. "My mother always did say I was just plain nosy. Shall I guess? You're trying to cure yourself of a childhood fear by making a pleasure trip."

"Not exactly. I'm going upriver to visit an old teacher of mine, a New Englander." That should make him think she was going all the way to Connecticut at least. "I haven't seen her for some time and I'm concerned about her." Now to use what Papa had said about the best defense being a prior attack. She snapped open her fan and looked over its top at him, remembering how Juliet had behaved in the ballroom scene. "Fair's fair, Mr. Tanner. It's my turn for questions. Why are *you* going upriver? A pleasure trip? Or on your way to studies somewhere? A Grand Tour?"

Carlton Tanner laughed. "Nothing so grand, unfortunately, though I wish it were. Actually, I'm on business for my father."

"Ah. Plantation business. Does your family have a large spread?" That was the sort of small talk the judge and his friends used with new acquaintances. If Carlton Tanner found it forward in a female, well, then he'd stop scraping acquaintance, and that was all to the good, wasn't it? She was surprised to find the thought made her rather lonely.

Carlton Tanner didn't seem a bit offended. "We're city people, actually. The Old Man has to travel quite a bit, so we don't own country property."

"How fascinating." Roxana fluttered the fan. "And what *does* he do? Are you one of the Virginia Tanners?" That should be safe. Southerners always talked family connections when they met, and most had kin somewhere in Virginia.

"I must be, mustn't I?" Carlton Tanner said blandly, as though he'd read her mind. His eyes twinkled. "My father's a procurement expert—not in trade, of course."

"Of course," Roxana replied, equally blandly. *He's a salesman*, she thought, amused, *and he doesn't want me to know it.*

She gazed with wide-eyed attention as Carlton Tanner went on. "He travels widely, and has many friends. If one of them is looking for certain merchandise, to buy, or reclaim, for example, the Old Man has a word here and there, and when he hears about a particular piece that's wanted—" He spread his hands.

"He passes the word?"

"Exactly! All quite easy and simple, you see, with the

advantages of wide travel and pleasant companions." He sketched a bow, then straightened. "And now, Miss Darden, as you said, fair's fair. I believe I'm allowed a question or two?"

"I won't promise to answer."

"Nor did I." Carlton Tanner bent toward her slightly, and his voice lowered, became more serious. "You could have traveled to New England overland. Your fear of the river is no childish fear. Yet you're traveling by boat, and not one of the grand large ones that you could have taken. There must be a reason stronger than a minor concern about the well-being of an old teacher. I'm right, am I not?"

To her shame, tears sprang to Roxana's eyes. She willed herself not to look away, and saw an abrupt change come over Carlton Tanner's face. He took out his pocket handkerchief, said, "Allow me," gruffly, and pressed it in her hand, then turned away.

"Thank you," Roxana whispered, and wiped her eyes. Golden Lad sat up, thrust his muzzle into her lap, and whined in sympathy. She stroked his ears, and the feel of them gave her courage. *Help me, God,* she thought, and took a deep breath.

"I can only say that my friend's—situation—is far from being a minor matter. It is very grave, enough so to . . . to necessitate my overcoming my very valid terror."

She heard Carlton Tanner catch his breath. "A boating accident," he said gently. "That's it, isn't it?"

"A few years ago . . . someone I cared for greatly was drowned. In this very river. An—accident on one of those grand safe boats you mentioned." Roxana swallowed and went on, sticking as close to the truth as she dared. "A friend of my elder brother. We had become quite close. Ever since, I've been terrified of drowning."

That at least was true, but as for the rest—She was telling one falsehood after another, and she'd been taught it was a sin to tell a lie. She hoped God would understand. It was all for Joss and Gideon Mapes, and God must hate slavery, considering what happened to the Israelites in Egypt.

There was a silence, during which Golden Lad whimpered again. Then Carlton Tanner, in a gentler voice than she could have imagined, said huskily, "Forgive me; I had no idea. My infernal curiosity forced you to speak of sacred memories. I assure you they will go no further."

He looked so shaken that impulsively, not knowing what else to do, she put out her hand. "Thank you kindly."

To her astonishment, instead of shaking it, he held it for a moment as she stared at him, wondering why her legs felt weak. "I cannot tell you how much I admire your courage in overcoming your fears, and how ashamed I am of my own conduct." His eyes looked straight into hers for a moment, as though he could read all the lies she'd told. Then he bent and kissed her hand.

He'd done that once before, but this was different. For a minute—it must have been the tight corset-lacing—Roxana thought she was going to faint. Face flaming, she snatched her hand away.

There was a moment's silence, then his voice said, in quite a different tone, "If I can be of service, call on me. Otherwise I shall not intrude again." He bowed and walked off with none of his usual self-confident stride.

Roxana, feeling as though she'd been wrung out and hung up to dry, went back to her empty stateroom.

"No harm done, and maybe some good. He'll think you've lost a sweetheart and are still mourning. That'll keep him from playing up to you, at any rate. I'd hate to get to heaven and have to explain to your mama why I let you flirt with a gentleman at age fourteen," was Joss's comment when she heard the story later.

"Once I get to Cincinnati I'll be *glad* to go back to being fourteen," Roxana said fervently.

EIGHT

Apparently talking about one's fears did help. Roxana did not dream that night.

The next day was Sunday, and Roxana awakened to the sound of a church bell ringing somewhere on shore. Joss climbed down from her bunk and peered out the window.

"Must be inland somewhere. There's nothing to see but woodlands, and it's not a pretty day."

Joss brought breakfast to the stateroom, along with news that morning worship would be held in the Main Saloon. Chairs were arranged in rows, in the very center of the boat, facing the Gents' Bar, which was tactfully concealed by a folding screen.

The service was conducted by a tall, bespectacled young man in a plain gray suit. "A seminarian returning to his studies at Lane Theological Seminary," Roxana heard a lady murmur to her neighbor. Lane Seminary! That was where Miss Hattie's father, the famous Dr. Lyman Beecher, presided. But in her role of "Miss Darden," Roxana dared not express any interest. She sat in a chair at the end of a row, right outside her stateroom door, with Golden Lad, at his own insistence, at her feet. The *Maria Q* had no melodeon, as larger boats often did, but Carlton Tanner unexpectedly produced a harmonica. He "set the tune" for the hymns quite creditably, and everyone joined in, including Golden Lad, who pointed his muzzle heavenward and keened. There were a few chuckles, but no one, including the seminarian, seemed to mind.

Dr. Beecher's seminary was a Presbyterian/Congregationalist institution, so the service was different from the Episcopalian one to which Roxana was accustomed. There was no Book of Common Worship with a set order of service and set prayers. Instead the seminarian just prayed "out of his head." He read some verses from Psalm 107:

They that go down to the sea in ships,
    that do business in great waters;
These see the works of the Lord, and his wonders in the deep.
For he commandeth, and raiseth the stormy wind,
    which lifteth up the waves thereof,
They mount up to the heaven, they go down again onto the
    depths:
    their soul is melted because of trouble. . . .
Then they cry unto the Lord in their trouble,
    and he bringeth them out of their distresses.
He maketh the storm a calm, so that the waves thereof are still.
Then are they glad because they be quiet;
    so he bringeth them unto their desired haven. . . .

"Their desired haven" . . . *that's what I want for Joss and Gideon,* Roxana thought. *That's what makes my bringing them to Cincinnati sort of a wedding gift, doesn't it?*

The New Testament reading, which provided the text for the brief sermon, came from First Corinthians Chapter 13. The part about charity was very familiar to Roxana. Miss Hattie, who had taught her Latin, had explained, as the seminarian did now, that the word *charity* came from *caritas*, and actually meant not almsgiving but caring. "Which means that it's not just *giving* charity that matters, but the caring behind it. Caring for even the least of these our brethren—the weakest, the most different, the most unloveable. Caring for those who are not like ourselves."

He didn't mention slavery, but suddenly the very word hung in the air. There was an uneasy rustling. Carlton Tanner, without warning, put his harmonica to his lips and began to tootle the familiar tune of Old Hundredth. With relief the congregation hauled itself to its feet and began to sing.

All people that on earth do dwell
Sing to the Lord with cheerful voice . . .

They sang it lustily, and the tension was released. That ended the worship service.

By now the sky had become a peculiar yellow gray, and a breeze had risen. Not enough to ripple the waters, which still were sluggish, but enough to promise storm.

Joss was looking out through the shutters when Roxana entered the stateroom. "Bad time comin'," she murmured, and rubbed her folded arms, exactly as Mam Lucy would have done.

"Don't you go getting all superstitious on me." Roxana muttered the words to herself, but somehow they slipped out into sound. Joss flashed her a startled glance.

"Ah'm not being superstitious. Ah'm merely pointin'

out we're due for a thunderstorm." That was what Joss said, but she spoke the words in an uncanny copy of Mam Lucy's own slurred dialect. Joss had been slipping more and more into that way of speaking as they neared Cincinnati, and it irritated Roxana.

"You don't have to speak like that when we're not in public, for goodness sake," she said.

"Like what, missy?"

"You know what! Like—like Mam Lucy."

"You mean like a po' ignorant fiel' han'?" Joss asked dangerously.

"I didn't say that!"

"Well, it's what you meant." Joss's dark eyes flashed. "You want me to act white, I'm going to act white and tell you a few things straight, Miss 'Alexandra Darden!' One, yes, I *do* have to speak like that, because it's what most of your people expect of me, and the closer we get to Cincinnati the more I'm afraid I'll slip and give Gideon away. Two, Mam Lucy may not have book learning, but she's far from stupid—"

"*I* know that!"

"—and I wouldn't have book learning either if it weren't for your dear mother. You see a poor, ignorant old servant when you look at Mam Lucy, much as you love her, don't you? *I* see what I'd have been if it hadn't been for your uncle's will! I just pray," Joss said grimly, rolling down her sleeves and tying on her kerchief, "that I can prove as strong as Mam Lucy is. Did you know she had two husbands and six children sold away from her? No, I didn't think you did. There's lots you don't know going on right under your nose. So you tend to your own pretend-acting for this trip, and let me tend to mine, or you'll sink us all!"

"Where are you going?"

"To spend Sunday with my husband, if you don't object," Joss retorted, and swept out.

Roxana was left feeling decidedly uncomfortable.

The trouble was, they both had headaches, partly from the barometric pressure and the heat, partly from nerves. Close as they were, they'd never spent days cooped up together in a cubicle five feet by eight.

The trouble was, Joss had been absolutely right in a lot she said.

Joss was not back when midday dinner was served, so Roxana went out to the main table. She sat between two elderly ladies, as far away from Carlton Tanner's unnerving presence as possible. Despite the effort of maintaining her "Miss Darden" role, she managed to sneak some food back to the stateroom, but Joss did not appear. Roxana put the food where Golden Lad couldn't steal it, and tried to read, but her head was throbbing, and the dog paced restlessly.

At last she slapped the book shut and put Golden Lad on his lead. At least out on deck there might be a breeze!

She stayed there most of the afternoon as clouds scudded overhead, increasingly dark. The lowering sun sent strange yellow rays out from behind those clouds. Her dress stuck to the skin between her shoulderblades, and Golden Lad paced and keened.

They were now much nearer to Cincinnati, and Joss had been right; every mile nearer increased, rather than lessened, tension.

"Boy seems restless. May I take him for a walk?"

Roxana jumped. Carlton Tanner stood before her, tipping his hat and speaking in a perfectly polite, quite formal tone. Apparently he meant to keep his word and not press acquaintance.

"Thank you. He would appreciate that very much."

Roxana handed over the leash and man and dog strode away, Golden Lad's tail waving like a banner. By the time they returned, raindrops were hitting the deck in slanting spurts. Carlton Tanner bowed and withdrew, and Golden Lad sat happily with his tongue hanging out trying to catch raindrops. A breeze had sprung up, but pressure was still heavy in the air.

At last it became too wet to stay outside. Roxana led Golden Lad back to the stateroom and Joss was there, changing out of clothes that were already soaked.

"Where you be, missy?" she demanded.

"I be walkin' on deck wid my boy, here, gettin' air." The words came out, of their own volition, in the thick dialect Joss had assumed as a disguise. *As if I were mocking— I didn't mean to, swear to God I didn't*, Roxana thought, appalled. But it was too late. Joss recoiled as though she'd been struck.

"Joss, I'm sorry! I didn't mean that the way it sounded!" Roxana rushed into speech. "It's my fool way of picking up other folks' accents, even when I don't mean to . . . I *know* I do it on purpose sometimes, like with Aunt Darden, but I didn't mean to now, swear to God . . . Mama always warned me I'd get in trouble for it someday. I'm so sorry. . . . Where have *you* been? I brought dinner back for you."

"I ate with Gideon." Joss's voice was muffled as she pulled clothes over her head.

"You shouldn't eat the stuff cooked down there! It's not fit to eat. I brought enough for you both. Why didn't you—"

"Because I wanted to eat with my husband," Joss said distinctly, buttoning her bodice. "That's more important to both of us than *what* we eat. We black folks can survive on pretty poor stuff, you know.''

"But there's no reason you have to—''

"Possum and coon can be mighty good eating if it's all you've got. Even if it's not. Mr. Mapes and I will be just fine, thank you, so you needn't worry whether we'll survive. So long as you don't go blurting out things you oughtn't, like a child play-acting to impress.''

"*What?*''

"I saw you standing talking with Mr. Carlton Tanner,'' Joss snapped. "Can't seem to stay away from each other nohow, can you?''

"*Oh, for heaven's sake!*'' Roxana swallowed and jerked her voice back to an undertone. "He offered to take Golden Lad for a walk. So I let him. We didn't *talk!* So you don't have to worry I did anything to give you and Mr. Mapes away. And you don't have to chaperone me. You're not my mother!''

Joss, to Roxana's horror, flinched again. "I've never presumed to think I was your mother,'' she said, too quietly. "I'm a poor black girl she was kind to, and I've tried to return that kindness, but I don't forget my place, don't you worry. And if I seem to, sometimes, well, you'll just have to put it down to us poor black folks not having the advantage of the finer shades of etiquette!''

Roxana stared. "What are you talking about? And why are you suddenly talking about 'us black folks' so much?'' Joss opened her mouth to speak, but Roxana rushed on. "Don't tell me about 'one drop of Negro blood,' because I know all that, and it's just silly. You *are* half white, and that's a fact, so why don't you ever think of yourself like that?''

"Sweet Jesus!'' Joss banged her hand down on the

dresser. "Why do you white people always assume we want to be white? We don't, you know. We just want what you whites take for granted. To be respected and free!"

"But you are! You're both. Just like you're both—"

Roxana was about to say *you're both black and white*, but she never got the chance. Joss was out of the stateroom, the door banging shut behind her. Roxana was left staring at the empty space where Joss had been.

You white people—Joss had never spoken like that before. Never spoken to *her* like that before. Why now?

The answer bounced back inside her brain. *Because she never felt free to. Because no matter what, she was still a servant. Because till now you never knew the truth about her. Because she's leaving.*

You white people— But I've never thought of myself as "white people," Roxana thought. Just as "people."

That was part of the trouble, wasn't it?

You white people— She'd understood, truly, why Joss had been "raised black," had had to think of herself as black. It had never occurred to her that Joss might be *proud* of being black. What did that say about Roxana herself?

Because she's leaving. Joss, who'd been with her every day, every night, except when she'd been off at school, would soon be gone. Weddings were romantic, the whole notion of her, Roxana, making possible Joss and Gideon's flight to safety was romantic. But it all came down to this one fact. At the end of the journey, Joss would be gone. Just as surely as, in a different way, Mama and brother George were gone. They were gone to God, and Joss and Gideon would be gone to Canada, most likely. And why? Because in these United States of America in the year 1836, Mr. and Mrs. Gideon Mapes couldn't really be respected and free, even if they both had freedom papers. In most places they couldn't even be legally married.

It's not fair, a part of Roxana's brain cried out childishly, and the other part answered, *Whoever promised you life was fair?* Not Mama, not Miss Hattie, not her father. The law troubles she'd overheard in his office should have taught her that.

But Joss is my cousin, the childish voice insisted, and back the answer came.

It makes no difference. And you never thought of Joss like that till now, any more than you thought of yourself as belonging to a race. Joss was just there for you.

I don't want to lose her!

The other voice was silent.

What will I do without her? Roxana wondered. *How could I have gotten through Mama's death without her? Why didn't I realize till now how much I love her?*

Because she, Roxana Grey, was selfish. Because she was blind. Because she was a child. Because she was white, and had made assumptions that suddenly, now, had been knocked all topsy-turvy.

Less familiar words from the Scripture she'd heard read that morning leapt suddenly to mind.

When I was a child, I spake as a child, I understood as a child, I thought as a child: but when I became a man, I put away childish things.

Never mind that she was just fourteen. By urging Joss and Gideon to make this trip, by taking responsibility for their flight to freedom, she had put away childish things, and must become a woman.

NINE

The stateroom reverberated with the silence of Joss's absence.

It was now quite dark, and despite the rain and slight breeze the heat was oppressive. Too hot for clothes like these. Roxana struggled out of her mother's dress, her mother's corset. *I never realized how much Joss has been helping me all along. I never realized a lot of things.*

It was suppertime. She could hear the clink of china and silver, the rise and fall of voices in the saloon. She didn't feel like eating, though there were leftovers from dinner in the cabin. Joss hadn't taken any away with her.

The thought of Joss and Gideon eating that bad food down below made her gag.

What would they do for food on their travels north? What would they do for money?

I never thought of any of that. All I thought of was getting them away to safety. No, correct that. All she'd really thought of was being the heroine leading them to safety. That was the blunt truth, wasn't it?

When I was a child, I spake as a child, I understood as a child, I thought as a child.

That's what she'd been doing, Roxana thought bitterly, when all the time she'd been thinking she was so grown-up. What had Joss called it? *Play-acting.*

Another line from the morning's Scripture reading crashed back into her mind . . . *now we see through a glass, darkly.* . . . It was Miss Catherine Beecher herself who'd explained once that *in a glass, darkly* really meant "in a looking-glass," a mirror. Roxana was seeing herself in a mirror right now, and she didn't like what she saw. Even less did she like the prospect of facing Joss. She had to apologize, she *wanted* to apologize, but what could she possibly say? *Excuse me for forgetting you'd been a slave? Excuse me for forgetting you had feelings?*

Joss, who'd been like a sister. Joss, who was a cousin. Joss, who was half of two races, and belonged to neither. Joss, who would soon be gone.

How about *Excuse me for not understanding any of this, before or now?* How about *I'm ashamed?*

Roxana got into her nightgown and lay down in the dark. Where was Joss now—sitting on sacks of peanuts with Gideon? Telling him what had happened? It came to Roxana with a jolt that she valued Gideon's good opinion and didn't want him to think badly of her.

Joss wouldn't stay down there all night, would she? The Main Deck couldn't be safe for women. And Joss and Gideon weren't really married. Except that jumping over the broom was all the marrying most black folks ever had. If that was all the laws allowed, then God must bless it, surely?

Roxana tossed and turned in the oppressive heat. Then,

abruptly, a wind rose, and the boat began to rock. An ominous rumble sounded in the distance, and lightning split the sky. Golden Lad's toenails scrabbled on the floor. He sat up, lifted his nose to the heavens, and wailed.

Suddenly thunder crashed like a hundred cannons. The heavens opened, and rain poured down in torrents. And with the rain came billows of cooling wind, and peace.

Roxana awoke to brilliant sunshine and a world new-washed. She stretched aching muscles, and looked around. The upper bed was empty. Either Joss had risen early and gone out . . . but she wouldn't have, not without taking Golden Lad with her for his morning walk . . . or she hadn't come back all night.

Golden Lad was sitting expectantly, leash in mouth and tail wagging madly. Roxana dragged herself up and, with some difficulty, made herself presentable in her mother's clothes. *Please, God, just don't let me bump into Carlton Tanner*, she prayed silently. She wasn't sure why the possibility made her feel so shaky, but it did. God must have listened, for the person she met in the sunlight of the gallery wasn't Carlton Tanner. It was Joss.

"Where were you? I was worried," Roxana blurted out.

"Gideon and I sat up all night talking. It was too hot for sleeping." Blessedly, there was neither defense nor attack in Joss's tone. "The roustabouts just told Gideon we'll be in Cincinnati in two hours."

Cincinnati! Impulsively, heedless of onlookers, Roxana hugged Joss. "Oh, I'm so glad! Then everything will be all right."

"I hope so, sugar," Joss said ambiguously, and hurried Roxana inside. The apology remained unspoken. The boat's crew was setting up for early breakfast and looked at them curiously as they passed. Joss switched quickly into humble manner and thick accent. "Dat's right, Miz Zan, you rest easy in youah stateroom while's ah fetch youah breakfast fo' you straightaway."

She slipped away while Roxana was still unlocking the stateroom door. And was back, with strawberries and melon, beaten biscuits and raspberry jam, before Roxana had found the words that must be said.

"Best eat quickly. No telling how soon we'll reach port." Joss set the tray beside Roxana and turned to start folding the garments hung on hooks.

Roxana wet her lips. "That can wait. Sit down, do! Unless you're going to eat below with Mr. Mapes—"

"Gideon said not to bother, as we'd be getting to Cincinnati soon."

"He can get a proper meal there. Cincinnati's not a southern city," Roxana said, knowing Joss would understand what she meant.

Joss nodded. "Gideon used to live here. He may still have friends here."

They were making small talk, unfamiliar and uncomfortable. *Joss doesn't want to risk another conversation like yesterday's either*, Roxana realized with a flash of insight. They were nearing safe haven. Perhaps that was enough?

The answer crashed into her mind with the suddenness of last night's crash of thunder. *No, it's not. Not when, God willing, Joss will be gone on the freedom train in a day or so.* She couldn't let Joss go, perhaps forever, with so much remaining unresolved.

She stared at Joss's straight back, at Joss's familiar hands folding Roxana's things in the same way that, through the years, she'd done so many unacknowledged services. The reality of never seeing Joss again was unbearable—

Golden Lad, sensing something, whined and thrust his muzzle insistently under Roxana's arm. Her hand jerked, and the plate of biscuits skidded. Golden Lad dove for them just as Roxana and Joss did also. Their heads banged together.

"I'm sorry—"

"I'm sorry—"

They both spoke at once. Golden Lad pushed his jam-daubed muzzle between them as they stared at each other. "Sit down!" Roxana said automatically. Golden Lad obeyed so promptly and virtuously that neither of the girls could keep from laughing. Their eyes met. Roxana took a deep breath. "You too," she said to Joss. "Sit down and eat, you hear?"

"Yes, ma'am," Joss responded, much in Golden Lad's manner, but her eyes were twinkling. She sat on the trunk and they finished what was left of the biscuits, fruit, and jam.

"Joss—"

"Let it be, Zan. This isn't the time or season. Too much to do."

"But I want to say—"

"I know what you want to say." Joss looked at Roxana directly. "We can talk, if need be, by and by. Right now, no need." Her smile flashed. "Now will you get that dog's face washed? Yours too. Unless you plan to go ashore with jam on your nose."

She sounded just as she always did, Roxana thought with relief. Then, with mixed joy and humility, she corrected herself. *Not "as always." As what she is: an older cousin.*

Farms and houses were now appearing along the riverbank, and the *Maria Q*'s horn acknowledged passing boats. Spectators began lining the gallery railings. "Gideon will see to the luggage once we dock," Joss said. "He says we should stay in here until we do."

By standing on the trunk Roxana could get quite a good look at the shoreline, despite the spectators in the way. At last the steeples of Cincinnati came into view. "Cincinnati has forty churches," Roxana said. "And there are colleges, and medical schools, and hospitals. And of course Lane Theological Seminary. That's Dr. Beecher's school. It's up in Walnut Hills. *Miss* Beecher's school's down in the city."

"Is that your Miss Hattie?" Joss inquired.

"Goodness, no! Miss Hattie's much younger, and nice, not at all scary. I thought you knew that."

"You've never talked about Cincinnati much, honey," Joss said gently.

"I guess I didn't, did I? I wasn't there for so very long. . . . It's a real city. Hotels, and theaters, and a Lyceum. Not that we schoolgirls were allowed to go to any of that! It's called the 'Queen City of the West.' And there's manufacturing—sawmills, paper mills, cotton mills." Roxana knew she was rambling. Perhaps it was impatience. Perhaps nervousness. Perhaps not wanting to remember the loneliness she'd felt when she'd first come, and the tragedy that caused her leaving—

Roxana got down off the trunk abruptly. She was already dressed in the dove-colored traveling outfit; now she put on her bonnet and tied it so it hid her eyes. "I think I will go up on deck, after all."

"Honey, not yet. It will be ages before we're tied up at dock, and there's a lot of cargo to be unloaded, Gideon says."

"I don't care. I want to be first ashore."

The sounds of the waterfront grew louder, and the

sounds of passing boats. The *Maria* Q returned each greeting with cheerful toots. At last they felt the boat jolting against the wharf. Roxana jumped up and grabbed Golden Lad's leash. "Come on," she ordered.

The saloons were nearly deserted, but passengers thronged the galleries. Roxana pushed through the crowd, in Golden Lad's wake, until she reached the stairs. There was chaos down on the Main Deck as roustabouts moved cargo about. She fought her way through until a deep voice, scandalized, said, "You oughtn't to be down here, missy."

Gideon Mapes, big and burly and looking like safe haven, grabbed Golden Lad's leash. He said "Down, boy!" firmly, and Golden Lad obeyed.

"I want to go ashore first," Roxana repeated, and Joss's voice behind her said, "I couldn't stop her."

Two roustabouts, pushing a pallet piled with logs, shouted profanely for them to move aside. Gideon sized up the situation and snapped out a whispered *"Come!"* He led the way swiftly through the moving maelstrom, with Roxana and Joss hurrying at his heels. Roxana overheard muttered oaths and insults. One white roustabout raised his fist; dropped it quickly when he spotted Roxana in the group. Somehow they managed to get ashore before any other passengers except two important-looking businessmen.

She was back in Cincinnati. Roxana stood, for the moment alone, on the hard-packed earth of the city's riverside plaza, feeling slightly dazed. She hadn't come by river before; she didn't know this part of Cincinnati. She certainly didn't know the smells! Behind her she heard Joss exclaim, "The luggage!" and Gideon answer in an undertone, "I'll go back for it. You keep those two *here*, and *with you*, understand?" Joss must have nodded. Roxana heard Gideon's feet running back towards the boat.

106

There was rattling and clattering back on the dock, but why was it so quiet here? Downtown Cincinnati on a weekday was, Roxana knew, a bustling place. This morning, in the whole of this riverside area stretching several blocks, no wagons rolled by, no horses pranced with riders or pulled stylish chaises.

"What *is* that smell? It's like rancid meat." Joss wrinkled her nose.

"I forgot. There are pork-packing plants along the river," Roxana said ruefully.

"Slaughterhouses, too, or I miss my guess. And breweries. The place stinks of likker." Joss glanced toward large warehouse-like buildings where black smoke rose from smokestacks.

The sun was shining, but a kind of invisible cloud hung in the air. *I don't remember it like this before*, Roxana thought uneasily. *And where are all the people?*

"Heah yo' be, Miz Darden," came Gideon's voice in his thickest, most humble accent. "Wheah yo' fixin' on us goin' naow?"

It struck Roxana forcibly that she didn't know where Miss Hattie lived. "We'll go to the school," she said aloud. "We'll hire a cab."

"Beggin' youah pardon, Miz Darden, but theah ain't no vehicles about." Gideon hoisted the trunk and Joss picked up the knapsacks. "Ah thinks we bettah walk."

They started off across the plaza, conscious of watching eyes along the shoreline.

Where *was* the school? Roxana was suddenly acutely aware that she'd never walked around the city alone. Cincinnati was laid out in a grid, with some roads running parallel to the river and others crossing them at right angles. Here was Main Street, wide and paved, with its modern sperm-oil lanterns hanging from carved wooden posts at each street corner. Here was Fourth and Sycamore and, at last, the building that housed Miss Catherine Beecher's school. It was closed and deserted. Roxana tried the door, tried to look through the blank windows with mounting alarm.

"What's wrong?" Gideon asked quietly, shifting the trunk's weight on his shoulders.

"I don't know. No one's here."

"Could be closed for summer," Joss suggested.

Of course. To her shame, Roxana's eyes filled with tears.

"You people looking for something?"

A tall, weatherbeaten man stood behind them, legs spread, arms folded. He looked Joss and Gideon up and down through narrowed eyes, then turned his attention to Roxana. "Strangers here, aren't you? I wouldn't recommend your wandering around. The climate's not too kindly just now."

He was clearly a gentleman, his manner was civil. *So why*, Roxana wondered, *am I afraid?* She drew herself up to her full height. "I am looking for Miss Harriet Beecher. I'm one of her former pupils. I thought to find her at the seminary."

The man's face softened slightly. "I'm sorry to say there's no Western Female Seminary anymore. There's no Miss Harriet anymore either. She's Mrs. Stowe now. Miss Catherine Beecher's gone traveling in the West. So you'd best hurry back to the docks—you've come by riverboat, haven't you?—and catch your boat again before she sails."

"But we can't—I mean, I *must* see Miss Hattie—it's why we came. It's a—a matter of life and death." The tears sprang up again, and she dashed them away.

To her astonishment, though the gentleman's eyes twinkled, his face looked approving. "You have spirit, don't you, young lady? Well, if you must see Mrs. Stowe, you'll find her out at Walnut Hills, at Dr. Beecher's house. I'd best drive you out."

"We'd be most grateful, if you know the way."

"Oh, I know it. I'm Mrs. Stowe's uncle, Samuel Foote, and it's very fortunate indeed that I ran into you. Come with me." Mr. Foote turned to Gideon Mapes. "You walk right beside me. And be quick."

He strode off. Gideon hoisted the trunk and fell in beside him. *Something's not right.* The thought flashed like lightning through Roxana's mind, but there was no time to question. She tucked her arm through Joss's and they hurried after the men.

Within minutes they were in a wagon and rattling up Montgomery Street toward Walnut Hills.

As the road climbed steeply the air grew clearer. They had left the city and were in real country now. Mr. Foote stopped at last before a substantial building of cream-colored brick. Behind were a barn, a brook, and virgin forest.

"You will be all right now. Forgive my not escorting you to the door. I must get back to town." Mr. Foote lifted his hat to Roxana. The gesture made his coat hang open, revealing a gun thrust through his belt. So something *was* wrong. "You'll be quite all right here," he repeated, with the faintest emphasis on the last word.

"You're sure Mrs. Stowe's at home—"

The man's leathery face softened and he almost chuckled. "Oh, yes, she's definitely here," he said. "Tell her I've seen her brothers, and they're fine," he added cryptically. The horse whinnied impatiently as Gideon helped Roxana and then Joss down. Then there was a quick slap of the reins, and the wagon went jolting off down the steep road.

Roxana knocked on the door.

It was several minutes before she heard footsteps come running. Then the door was half-opened and a white-skinned hired girl peered out blankly. The blankness turned to fear as she took in Gideon Mapes's color and size.

"Dr. Beecher ain't home," she said abruptly and started to withdraw.

Without even thinking Roxana thrust her foot between the door and doorjamb. "It's Miss Hattie we've come to see—I mean, Mrs. Stowe. I'm a former student." To her relief the hired girl backed inside slightly, and Roxana followed. "You come too," she threw back over her shoulder.

Somehow they were all inside. Somehow the door was shut. "Who shall I say's callin'?" the hired girl asked, and Roxana started, unsure which name to use. And then there was the tap of feet hurrying along an upper corridor and on the stairs, and a remembered voice called breathlessly, "Is it Henry—Oh!"

Roxana swung round, and the words of greeting died on her lips. The tiny figure that had stopped halfway down the stairs was swollen, and the heavy-lidded, blue gray eyes were alarmed and puzzled. *Miss Hattie's having a baby,* Roxana realized, startled. *And she doesn't know me!*

"Miss Hattie, it's me!" she blurted. "Roxana Grey."

"Roxana?" Harriet Beecher Stowe peered down doubtfully.

"The hair," Joss whispered.

Of course! Hurriedly Roxana untied and removed her bonnet. "It's really me, Miss Hattie—I mean Mrs. Stowe—"

To her relief she saw Miss Hattie's eyes light with their old warmth. "Zan, dear! What a nice surprise! How elegant you've grown! And how tall! And whatever have you done with your hair?''

"We had to dye it so I'd not be recognized. I'm so sorry to burst in on you, and at a time like this—" Roxana jerked her gaze from Miss Hattie's waistline. "This is my . . . my friend Joss. And her husband, Gideon Mapes. Papa's away, and the next stationmistress is also, and we didn't know where else to go—"

"I'm an escaped slave, Mrs. Stowe," Gideon Mapes cut in quietly, his thick accent entirely gone. "I had reason to think a bounty hunter had located me. My . . . wife wouldn't let me leave without her, and the countryside around Grey's Landing wasn't safe. Miss Grey came up with the plan to come north by river, posing as a southern woman with her slaves."

"By river." That was all Mrs. Stowe said, but her glance to Roxana spoke volumes.

Roxana swallowed. "It was all I could think of. *You* were all I could think of. I knew the Beechers are Anti-Slavery, and I thought . . . I didn't know about your being married and . . . everything." She blushed. "Anyway, I knew they'd be safe in Cincinnati," she finished in a small voice.

There was a split-second silence. Then, to Roxana's bewilderment, Mrs. Stowe burst into laughter. One hand pressed to her waist, the other clutching the stair rail, she laughed until she hiccupped, and Joss ran to lead her down. Joss steered Miss Hattie into the front parlor and down onto a chair. Roxana, seeing the hired girl hovering in the rear corridor, ordered her to fetch a glass of water.

"Milk, and four glasses," Miss Hattie corrected between hiccups. "And ask Miss Beecher please to fry up a mess of eggs and bacon. I'm sure these folks haven't had a decent breakfast. . . . I'm sorry," she gasped when the hired girl had vanished. "It was that word, *safe*. You obviously don't know that for the past few weeks Cincinnati's been in the grip of a 'nigger-hunting' mob!"

TEN

The words hung in the air as Roxana froze, and Gideon looked at Joss, who was kneeling at Miss Hattie's side. She rose quickly. "It's *all right*, Zan," Joss said in an undertone. "Mr. Mapes has friends in the city. We'll find a place—"

"Stuff and nonsense, Mrs. Mapes!" Miss Hattie's voice rang out. "Of course you'll stay here, and of course we'll help you! And I hope you don't think that dreadful phrase was mine! It's the term being used—by certain young *gentlemen* from our best families and their riffraff followers—for what's become their favorite summer sport!"

"But this is a *northern* city!" Roxana exclaimed in shock.

"Ah, but Kentucky's right across the river," Miss Hattie retorted. "Cincinnati's a great river port, remember. And this time of year all the 'southern buyers' are in town. This is a dangerous time for political disturbances. Particularly when most of the clergy are away for the annual denominational meetings! Oh, how I wish Father were here!" she added. "Although, knowing him, he might have gotten himself killed last night. I only hope my brothers haven't."

Roxana gasped. "I forgot! A Mr. Samuel Foote—"

"You know Uncle Samuel?"

"He drove us here. From the dock. He said to tell you he'd seen your brothers, and they're fine."

"Oh, thank God." Miss Hattie folded her hands against her chin and closed her eyes briefly. "I'm sorry," she murmured, opening them again. "I'm a bit shaky these days—"

The front door slammed.

Miss Hattie swung around as fast as her condition would permit. "That must be my brother! He'll know what's happened—" A handsome young man with eyes like hers dashed past the parlor doorway. *"Henry, wait!"*

"Not now, Hattie! No time to lose." He vanished into the back regions of the house.

"He could at least have told us what's going on in town," Miss Hattie sputtered. "I do beg your pardon. Now, where were we?"

In the back of the house, somebody shrieked.

The scream was followed by a loud bang, and the sound of raised voices, and then the hired girl came rushing in.

"Oh, Miz Stowe, Miz Stowe! He's ruining Miss Beecher's good coffeepot and she's all upset—"

"What?" Miss Hattie, with surprising agility, hauled herself to her feet. Followed by Roxana, Joss, and Gideon, she dashed to a large, well-equipped kitchen. A fire blazed in the iron cookstove. Beside it sputtered a middle-aged lady, with frying pan in hand and outraged face. The young man, jacket off and shirtsleeves rolled, was stirring something in a zinc coffeepot that gave off a noxious smell. A tray with milk pitcher and glasses stood, forgotten, next to some metal molds on the bare wood table.

"It's all right, Aunt Esther, I'll take care of this. I think you'd better go supervise that girl before she scrubs a hole in the floorcloth Mama painted. She never does things properly if you're not there to oversee," Miss Hattie added artfully. As soon as the older woman had hurried out, she shut the door, jammed the back of a chair beneath the knob to keep it shut, and whirled around. "Henry, what on earth are you doing?"

The young man didn't even look up. "Making bullets, Hattie."

Miss Hattie gasped. "What for?"

"To kill men with. Don't slow me down, Hattie. The mayor's called for a corps of volunteers to police the city. He's sworn me in with orders to shoot to kill, if necessary."

Gideon Mapes began rolling up his sleeves. "I'm a blacksmith. I know about casting metal."

"Good, because I don't, really," Miss Hattie's brother said. "Find another pot and start melting those lead bars over there."

Miss Hattie sprang forward. "That's Aunt Esther's preserving kettle!" She found a battered pot on a lower shelf and handed it to Gideon. "Miss Grey, Mrs. Mapes, Mr. Mapes, this is my brother Henry Ward Beecher. I have no intention of trying to slow you down, Henry, since I know quite well that's impossible. I may, however, kill *you* if you don't tell us what's happened overnight!"

"What do you know so far?" Henry asked Gideon, who shook his head. "Naught? Then list, oh list!"

"Stop being dramatic, Henry, and spit it out," Miss Hattie ordered.

Henry smiled without humor. "In plain English, another riot. The same young 'gentlemen' and their scurvy cohorts who tried to stop publication of the *Philanthropist* three weeks ago—Abolition newspaper," he explained in an aside to the visitors, "—decided to go back this weekend and finish the job." He straightened, so quickly that hot lead splashed out of the coffeepot onto the kitchen table.

"*Careful!*" Gideon took the pot out of Henry's hands.

"Sorry." Henry grinned sheepishly. "Maybe I'd better melt and you pour. Write down what I say to you, Hattie. Make it into an editorial for the *Journal*. I won't have time to compose one, that's for sure. She's been writing editorials for some time, actually," he said grandly to the others. "Only she disguises them as Letters to the Editor. In dialogue form. One of these days this sister of mine will be a famous lady novelist, you mark my words!"

Miss Hattie, about to begin frying eggs in a huge black fry pan, surrendered it to Joss and sat down at the center table. Pens, paper, and a capacious inkpot already stood there, and she pulled them toward her quickly. "Henry's temporary editor of the Anti-Slavery newspaper," she explained to the others proudly. "His editorials have been considered 'well-studied, earnest and dignified.'"

It was hard for Roxana to imagine the impetuous Henry Ward being dignified. He was too much like Golden Lad who, overlooked in the general excitement, had thrust his head into the flour barrel and now was sneezing. Miss Hattie laughed, Joss jerked the fry pan to one side and grabbed the dog, and Gideon opened the back door and thrust him out. Roxana, torn between embarrassment and the giggles, struggled to maintain decorum. She hadn't realized how tired she was. Or how worried. Now that she was here at last, giddiness had set in. Between Golden Lad's enthusiasm, and Miss Hattie's brother—

She was suddenly, uncomfortably conscious that Miss Hattie's brother was looking straight at her and had read her mind. Only his gaze was neither annoyed nor amused; it was admiring. He winked as though they shared a secret. Roxana dropped her eyes swiftly, heat flooding through her.

"Have a glass of milk, Miss Roxana," Henry's voice said solemnly, a hint of a laugh behind it. "Very good for the vapors."

"I'll vaporize you if you don't start dictating," Miss Hattie said pointedly.

Roxana sat, not looking up again. Joss fried eggs and ham and served them, and they ate, and all the time the bullet making and the talk about slavery went on.

Cincinnati was violently divided on the subject, Henry and Miss Hattie explained. There were Pro-Slavery, Anti-Slavery (gradual abolition), Abolitionist (instant abolition) and Repatriation (return the blacks to Africa) factions. There were newspapers representing each of these groups, the *Philanthropist* being Abolitionist and the *Journal* Anti-Slavery.

"And there's rivalry between the papers," Roxana murmured. Not for nothing had she listened to her father's comments on the combustible mixture of partisan politics and the press.

Henry's jaw dropped, and his hand stopped in midair. "Good for you, Miss Roxana! And when you throw in the fact that the *Philanthropist*'s Methodist, and the *Journal* Presbyterian—"

"My father's always said there's more ways than one that religion and politics don't mix well in a democracy," Roxana said. Then she blushed and dropped her eyes at the sudden flare of admiration she saw in his.

Henry went on dictating to Miss Hattie, comparing events to "flame jets which never come unpursued by the earthquake." Racial tension had been festering for some

117

time, it seemed. The presence of the southern buyers had provided a spark, and Abolition editorials had fanned the flame. After an Anti-Abolition riot several days ago, three prominent citizens—a noted law professor, the editor of the conservative daily *Gazette*, and a young attorney named Salmon Portland Chase—called a meeting to cool the tension. Anti-Abolition forces had packed the meeting and roared the moderates down. A spontaneous gathering crowded into the Lower Market and organized a committee to warn the editor of the Abolition paper to leave town.

"He told the committee what they could do with their warning," Henry said with relish. "The committee thereupon published their abhorrence of violence, and their warnings to the populace to abstain therefrom, and then washed their hands of the whole thing."

"But the populace didn't abstain," Gideon said knowingly. Henry nodded.

"When weekend came, the mob, still with the young *gentlemen* at its head, gathered at Seventh and Main and howled threats at 'damned Abolitionists' while the mayor watched 'em from his window." Henry's face darkened. "Then came yesterday. Sunday. Dead hot. Foreboding. All people of color vanished from the streets. They knew a storm was coming."

Roxana nodded. "We had it on the river. Closeness, then thunder and lightning, then the rain."

"The liquid here in Cincinnati was likker," Henry Ward said bluntly. "The mob got likkered up, then went back to the printing house and destroyed the press. The mayor showed up, congratulated them on a job well done, and told them to go home. Instead they went looking for Birney, the editor of the *Philanthropist*, who lives at the Franklin House hotel."

"Did they get him?" Miss Hattie demanded. Henry Ward shook his head.

"They *got* Salmon Portland Chase! Wish I'd seen it," Henry said admiringly. "Not much older than I am, from the best families back East, richer than rich, lawyer for two of the city's biggest banks—Chase's never even *met* Birney. But he barred the door of the Franklin House and told the mob it could not pass. He told them *he* could be found at any time, if they wanted action. *Then* the mayor came out and said that Birney wasn't there."

"And they left?"

"Yep! Went back to the printing house and wrecked what was left. Then they went 'nigger hunting' in the Church Alley slum. Somebody let off a couple of shots, so they stampeded for refuge into another hotel, had a few more rounds of drinks, convinced themselves that one of their lot must have been killed—which wasn't true—and went back to Church Alley looking for revenge. All the Negroes who are usually there had fled, so the mob had to be satisfied with just wrecking the shacks." Henry Ward glanced at Gideon briefly. "The only law force Cincinnati has is a night watch. One captain, six patrolmen. Hence the volunteer militia." He picked up one of the now-hardened bullets, loaded it into his pistol, and cocked it.

"If I can be of use—" Gideon said.

Roxana saw Joss repress a shudder, but not speak. She herself straightened and took a deep breath.

"*We* have guns, Mr. Beecher. Two of them. And bullets."

ELEVEN

Miss Hattie, Henry Ward Beecher, and Gideon Mapes swiveled to stare at her.

Roxana stared back. "They're my father's pistols. He taught Joss and me target shooting. Before he left for Washington, he told me most particularly to remember the guns. He meant us to use them if necessary."

"You brought them with you?" Miss Hattie asked calmly. The two men both looked stunned.

Roxana nodded. "One's in the trunk. The other's here." She opened the heavy bag hanging from her wrist and brought out the gun. Joss's jaw dropped.

"Sugar, you didn't tell me."

"I didn't want you any more worried than you were," Roxana confessed. She laid the gun on the kitchen table, and there was a silence as they all stared at it, looking so harmless with its mother-of-pearl-inlay handles and pretty engraving.

Roxana looked at Gideon briefly. "I'll just bet Mr. Mapes has a gun with him, too."

Gideon didn't answer, but a glance passed between him and Henry.

"I still don't know," Miss Hattie said pointedly, "what's happening in town this morning."

"Nothing, yet." Henry Ward emptied his own pistol and set it down next to Roxana's. "But make no mistake, Hattie, this is a city under siege. The mob may have slunk off to its dens, but no one can predict how long they'll stay there. One incident could set the violence off again."

Gideon frowned. "Then we cannot impose upon your kindness and risk your safety by staying here."

"*Oh, yes, you will!*" Miss Hattie said firmly. "You'll stay till the danger's over, and then my brothers, and Uncle Sam Foote too, if needed, will see you and your wife off safely on—what did Roxana call it? The Underground Railroad. We have plenty of room here at the moment. You and your wife can have Dr. Beecher's room."

Roxana saw Joss and Gideon exchange glances, then Joss dropped her eyes. "I usually sleep in Miss Zan's room," she murmured.

"We've not had a proper wedding yet, Mrs. Stowe," Gideon said quietly. "Judge Grey's approved our pledge, but he had to leave Grey's Landing with no time for nothing. Then I found out my old master was looking for me, and Joss wouldn't let me leave without her. We've only been able to jump over the broom. We want to have a proper Christian wedding."

"I understand perfectly," Miss Hattie said, tears glistening in her eyes. "One thing we have plenty of around here is ministers. I gather that you're both professing Christians?" Gideon and Joss both nodded. "Then there'll be no barrier to your being wed in a religious ceremony. Mrs. Mapes shall stay with Zan in Father's room, and we'll make your bed elsewhere. My brothers shall find a minister to marry you. In our parlor, where Mr. Stowe and I were married. And you shall most certainly," she added, "stay with us until it's safe for you to leave!"

There was no further discussion on the subject. Henry Ward finished making his bullets and went back downtown. He refused to let Gideon accompany him. "You owe it to your bride not to get yourself killed before the ceremony."

"What about you?" Roxana couldn't help asking.

"Nobody'd kill me," Henry Ward said grandly. "They'd be too afraid of Father!" He marched out, whistling.

Miss Hattie watched him leave, almost regretfully. "If I were a man, I would go. As it is, I must content myself with writing." She took a deep breath and reached for pen and paper.

The rest of the day passed quietly. Miss Hattie told Joss about her own wedding, which had been small and quiet. "Altogether domestic," she said, smiling. "Nobody present but my own brothers and sisters, and a fellow teacher as my maid of honor. As there was a sufficiency of the ministry in my family, we did not even have to call upon the aid of an outside pastor! My only regret is that sister Catherine was away, so she could not witness my departure from her care and guidance to another's."

"I wish I'd been here," Roxana exclaimed.

Miss Hattie's eyes twinkled. "I'm afraid you'd have been disappointed. It was all done and over before any of the numerous friends and acquaintances who took such deep interest in matchmaking even knew about it."

"I thought you'd have had a big, splendid wedding," Roxana said ruefully.

"Oh, no, my dear, I'd have been far too self-conscious! I was already totally bewildered. Here I scarcely knew who

Hattie Beecher was, and now I was about to turn into no-body knows who!" She turned to Joss. "Do you know, I lay awake all the week before, wondering how I should live through this overwhelming crisis, and do you know what I felt when the time came? *Nothing at all!*"

It sounded absolutely crazy to Roxana, but she saw Joss nod.

"You too?" Miss Hattie asked.

Joss dropped her eyes. "We've been . . . walking out all this spring. Along the river, and talking. He's so kind, and strong— Not just outwardly. Inside. He *understood* about me." She didn't explain what she meant, and Miss Hattie didn't ask, just put one small hand over Joss's and squeezed it. After a moment Joss went on. "He'd just asked if he could ask the judge's permission to marry me, and then the judge was gone, and within weeks all this happened."

"If I may be allowed to say so, I think you will be happy together," Miss Hattie said gently. "Even a stranger can see that you can *trust* each other. That means a great deal."

They sat in companionable silence in the parlor, as a cool piney breeze drifted in from the forest to cut the day's heat. At Miss Hattie's suggestion, they ate a picnic lunch under the trees. During the afternoon Miss Hattie rested, and Aunt Esther fussed over the hired girl's preparations for dinner. She had been introduced to the unexpected guests, and accepted their presence matter-of-factly. Then Henry came home, bringing with him his younger brother Charles and several newspapers which he flung on the parlor table with a flourish.

"Wait till you see what Hammond of the *Gazette* has done! Not a word of reporting or editorial comment on the mobocracy! He's simply published the entire Sermon on the Mount!"

"The Beatitudes could do a lot of people a peck of good," Aunt Esther commented.

From the kitchen regions a gong sounded, and the hired girl's voice called loudly, *"Dinner!"*

"I do wish you could cure her of that, Aunt," Miss Hattie murmured, and Miss Beecher responded wryly, "Don't think I haven't tried."

Their voices sounded unnaturally commonplace, for a tension had suddenly descended. Not on the Beechers—on Roxana, Joss, and Gideon. *Where were Joss and Gideon supposed to eat?* Roxana wondered. Would that white hired girl want them eating with *her?*

Through the uneasy turmoil in her brain she heard Miss Hattie's voice say, quite normally, "Mr. Mapes, will you escort me in?"

For the first time since she'd known him Roxana saw Gideon taken aback. "Beg pardon, Mrs. Stowe, but that wouldn't be proper, surely."

"Certainly it would. You are our guests, and as Aunt Esther graciously defers to my married state and lets me preside over the table while I'm staying here, you shall sit at my right hand. And Henry shall have the pleasure of Miss Grey and Mrs. Mapes on either side at the other end— a prerogative I'm quite sure Dr. Beecher would claim for himself if he were here. Now do come along, Mr. Mapes," Miss Hattie said impishly, "for I assure you I can use a strong arm to lean on, and the food is getting cold."

Dinner was an experience. The food was good, but the talk was dominant. And table talk at the Beechers was like nothing Roxana had ever encountered. *Papa would enjoy it,* she thought. A spirited, rapid-fire discussion of current events took place, complete with debate on the theological, practical, and political ramifications. Theology books, the Bible, and even newspapers were brought to the table and quoted.

It was no surprise that slavery, and the situation along the Ohio–Kentucky border, was the primary subject. Miss Hattie, when her brothers allowed a lull in the rapid-fire debate, tried to draw the visitors into the discussions. Only Gideon responded, with quiet dignity, citing both Biblical passages and real-life experience to make his points. Joss kept silent and looked at no one, and Roxana held her tongue for fear she'd say too much. But the Beechers were eager to hear what Gideon could tell them, and soon Roxana could sense both Joss and Gideon relaxing their guard.

Presently the conversation reached the subject of the slave catchers and slave auctions. Roxana saw Joss flinch and drop her eyes. "It's a comfort at least to know that slave selling in the North is rare," Aunt Esther put in, trying vainly to lower the intensity level. "Certainly no God-fearing Christians—"

"Beg pardon, Miss Beecher, but that's just not so," Gideon interrupted. "It does happen. All the time."

Involuntarily Roxana glanced at Joss, but Joss was sitting like a statue, staring at her hands. She felt Henry Ward looking at her shrewdly, and saw his eyes travel to Joss also. Blessedly, he didn't ask her any questions. Instead he turned to Roxana, his eyes twinkling.

"How about you, Miss Roxana? Surely a lady with the brains and spirit to devise the brilliant strategy of your current trip has something to contribute about this country's 'peculiar institution'! One would think you were still a shy schoolgirl in my sisters' classrooms!"

Roxana felt her cheeks growing scarlet.

"Let her alone, Henry!" Miss Hattie came to her rescue. "She's never experienced the onslaught of a Beecher 'disputation'! That's what Father calls these debates," she explained. "He brought us up on them, to teach his sons how to argue theology, and prepare them for the ministry, which to him is no placid calling. And of course, sister Catherine learned too!"

"Are you saying you didn't, Hattie?" Henry Ward asked slyly. "The only difference is that you employ your passion in writing your dialogues on paper and calling 'em Letters to the Editor!" That won a round of general laughter. "Anyway," he finished, "Father just loves a good argument. All Beechers do!"

After dinner things quieted down. There were family prayers, and then music. Charles Beecher, who was musical, played the melodeon and they all sang hymns.

It had been a day of calm before storm. Through Monday, Tuesday, and Wednesday, Cincinnati held its breath. The night watch patrolled, augmented by the volunteer militia which also patrolled by day. The *Gazette* published first the Constitution of Ohio, then the Declaration of Independence, without comment. Finally it came out with what Miss Hattie called "a simple, concise history of the mob," telling its whole history, and naming names.

In Walnut Hills, several hundred feet above the city, the pattern of Beecher life went on. Henry Ward went off with the volunteer militia, and Charles went wherever he did go, Miss Hattie wrote, and everyone came together for dinner and disputation, prayers and music. No one spoke of Joss and Gideon's dilemmas, at least not to them or before Roxana, although Roxana suspected conferences were going on in private.

At last, before dinner on Friday, Miss Hattie called her

guests together in the parlor. Henry Ward was sitting there, looking unnaturally solemn and full of secrets.

"What's happened?" Roxana asked apprehensively.

"Sit down, please, all of you. Nothing's 'happened'," Miss Hattie said calmly, "but we do have some news for you, and some—recommendations."

She turned to Henry, who cleared his throat.

"You can be married here tomorrow, if you like. I've spoken to a minister friend, and it's all arranged."

Joss let her breath out in relief. Gideon's eyes narrowed.

"That is very fine, and we appreciate it. But what happens to us then? We cannot impose on your kindness here forever."

Henry Ward and Miss Hattie exchanged glances. Then Miss Hattie straightened, and seemed literally to grow taller. She looked straight at Roxana. "We have looked into all possibilities and consulted Abolitionist friends. The slave hunters are likely to continue raids through the border states all summer. It's worse than usual this year, because of political events you do not know of—"

That's why Papa took off for Washington, Roxana thought with sudden insight.

"—so we are all agreed that your best route to freedom is your original plan—to continue your masquerade, and go on the river again."

Roxana gave an involuntary exclamation.

Miss Hattie's great blue gray Beecher eyes were looking clear into Roxana's soul. "It was a truly God-given idea, and you carried it through nobly and with great courage. Clearly, no one suspected your false identities. If you can carry it through again, and go to Pittsburgh—"

"*Pittsburgh!*"

"That is definitely a northern city and, like Cincinnati,

a river crossroads. More important, traveling overland will be safe for you from there. It will be possible for you to go straight to Canada in a short space of time," she said, turning to Joss and Gideon. "I myself will write to Judge Grey and give him all the particulars. If the letter goes out tomorrow, he should be able to travel by fast stage and join you aboard the steamboat in Marietta." Marietta, Ohio, was on a straight line west of Washington, DC.

Roxana steeled herself and nodded.

At the dinner table that night the talk was all of the wedding and the trip upriver. Charles would inquire about steamboat schedules. "For Monday," Miss Hattie warned. "There could be trouble in town over the weekend."

Henry would consult their uncle Samuel Foote to learn locations of Underground Railroad agents who would help Joss and Gideon on their way north. Miss Hattie would write letters of introduction they could carry with them.

"What music would you like for your wedding?" Charles Beecher asked.

Joss came to with a start. "What? Oh . . . whatever you think."

"*Over Jordan*," Roxana said.

Charles smiled. "Not exactly traditional for a wedding, but why not?"

"That's enough planning for one evening," Miss Hattie said, rising. "The bride's overwhelmed, and I don't blame her. You gentlemen can work on the rest of the details, but we ladies shall make it an early night. Come along, my dears."

She led the way upstairs, but tactfully left Joss and Roxana to themselves. They puttered around the bedroom, scarcely speaking. Roxana took off her dress and corset, put on a wrapper, and began to undo her hair. The unaccustomed braids and curls were tangled, and she groaned. Joss came over and took the brush out of Roxana's hands, as she'd done so many times over the years.

"You won't be doing that much longer," Roxana murmured. She meant it to sound light and teasing, but it came out sad.

There was a tap on the door and Miss Hattie's head peeped round it. "May I come in?" She too had changed into nightgown and wrapper and looked tinier than ever with her hair down her back. "I want to apologize if we let our Beecher enthusiasm run away with us," she said, taking one of Joss's hands in each of hers. "Believe me, I know how overwhelming a wedding can be."

"We're getting married, not 'having a wedding,' " Joss said, shaking her head slightly.

"How wise of you to recognize which is the important thing. All the same, we must make it a memory to last a lifetime. What shall you wear?"

"What I've been wearing," Joss said briefly. "Slaves wouldn't travel with grand wardrobes."

Miss Hattie's face fell. "And I'm much too short for anything of mine to fit you. I should have realized . . . I've been tactless, and I'm so sorry. It was my foolish hope that you'd at least have that, since you have no family to be with you."

There was a momentary silence. Then Roxana heard a voice out of nowhere say, *"Oh, yes, she does!"*

It was her own voice, speaking out as it had when she'd proposed the river expedition.

"Zan, don't." That was Joss's voice, alarmed.

Roxana shook her head. "I'm going to tell, Joss, no matter what." She took a deep breath and turned to Miss Hattie. "Joss is my cousin. Uncle Darden was her father. I just found it out in her freedom papers, but I always *knew* she was kin, just not by blood."

"I thought it was something like that," Miss Hattie nodded, not looking the least bit shocked. "It's not an unusual story." Something in her tone made Joss look at her sharply.

"And I know what she's wearing to be married in." Roxana ran to the trunk and began throwing things out until she came to her mother's dinner dress of white silk mull. "Take it. Keep it. You can have the rest of them, too, once we get to Pittsburgh, except for what I need to travel home. You won't need to pose as slaves once you get to Pittsburgh, Mr. Beecher as good as said so. And here!" She held the sewing bag upside down over the trunk until the thick roll of United States currency and the gold coins rolled out.

Behind her, both Joss and Miss Hattie gasped. Roxana was too busy to pay attention, counting the bills out into two equal piles. She rolled one up and held it out to Joss. "It's your dowry. Take it. I know Papa would say you should."

Joss drew back as though stung. "I can't!"

"Yes, you can! Call it wages, if you must. Or call it your freedom money, which Uncle Darden should have had the decency to leave for you! You know Papa would have spent this or more to buy your freedom, if Uncle hadn't left you to Mama. Use it to buy Gideon's freedom, if you need to. But just take it!"

"I think you should," Miss Hattie said calmly. "Roxana was right. You *are* kin, even if there hadn't been any common blood. I think you've both been blessed." She took the money from Roxana's hands, pressed it into Joss's, and held them. "I was going to take the prerogative of seven months of wifehood to preach you a sermon on marriage, but I think I'll just share with you my motto, which Uncle Sam taught me and Mr. Stowe confirmed for me. *Horas non numero nisi serenas.* 'Number—' ''

'' 'Number no hours that are not serene' . . . count only the happy hours,'' Joss finished.

Miss Hattie's face lit up. ''You know Latin!''

''Roxana's fath—'' Joss started, and then stopped. ''My aunt and uncle Grey had me well taught.''

TWELVE

Joss and Gideon were married in the Beecher parlor on Saturday afternoon. It was the first real wedding Roxana had attended and she found it, though quiet, deeply moving. Miss Hattie and Roxana had filled the room with flowers, and Miss Hattie herself prepared a bouquet of white blossoms for Joss and another of blue for Roxana. It seemed taken for granted by the Beechers that Roxana would "stand up" for Joss, and Henry Ward had appointed himself Gideon's best man. All the Beechers, and Uncle Sam Foote, appeared for the ceremony, dressed in Sunday-go-to-meeting clothes. Gideon was dignified and handsome in one of the great Dr. Lyman Beecher's own black broadcloth suits. The minister was tall, bespectacled, polite, and young.

The wedding moved through its Presbyterian Order of Worship course. Charles Beecher played music by Handel beforehand, and then everyone sang a hymn. Joss, at Gideon's request, sang *Deep River*. It wasn't until mid-service that there was a pause. "Who giveth this woman to be married to this man?" the minister asked, and everyone looked around.

"I guess *I* do," Roxana said at last. "On behalf of Judge Grey, my father." *And your uncle,* her eyes said to Joss, but Joss was looking only at Gideon.

Henry Ward had offered to go downtown and buy a wedding ring, but Joss had unexpectedly refused. Instead, at her request, Gideon placed his own hoop earring of African gold upon her finger. After the ceremony there was a wedding collation beneath the trees, with fruit punch and the wedding cake Aunt Esther had personally baked. The breeze was full of the scents of flowers and of pine. Golden Lad had been tied up during the ceremony itself, but he had keened along with the singing, making everyone smile.

That night Joss and Gideon occupied Dr. Beecher's bedroom, and Roxana shared with Miss Hattie. It was the first time they had had private time together.

"You're really going to miss her, child, aren't you?" Miss Hattie asked as they prepared for bed. Roxana nodded, her eyes filling.

"Joss has always been there. Especially since Mother—"

"I know, dear, I know. I was just five when my mother died of galloping consumption. After that, sister Catherine, who was sixteen, became my mother."

"I guess Joss has been mine, these past two years," Roxana said humbly. "I never realized till just lately how much she's been and done."

"That's often the case, unfortunately," Miss Hattie agreed. "The good part is that it makes us learn to appreciate people while we have them. And after a while the pain of losing those who've gone turns into happy memories." She paused. "I remember being dressed in black for Mama's funeral, the slow walk to the burying, and the ring of solemn people around the grave. But do you know what I remember most? The time earlier when I found a sack of what I thought were onions in the nursery cupboard, and persuaded little Henry that we should eat them. Small children weren't allowed to eat onions, which convinced us they must be especially good!''

"Were they?" Roxana asked curiously.

Miss Hattie shook her head. "They tasted odd. Which was not surprising, because they weren't onions at all, but tulip bulbs, expensive and rare, that a seafaring uncle had sent to Mama." She was silent for a moment. "Mama must have been devastated, but I'll never forget the expression on her face when she caught us just after the crime. Not even a momentary impatience, just fleeting sadness as she explained that now there would be no beautiful red and yellow flowers in the garden come spring. . . . I hope I'll have as much patience when *I'm* a mother!''

"You will," Roxana said positively.

"One morning soon after Mama's funeral," Miss Hattie went on, "sister Catherine looked out the window and found Henry digging in the yard. When she asked why, he informed her he was going down to visit Mama and God! Since Mama's coffin had been buried, he assumed that heaven must be under ground!''

When I was a child, I thought as a child, I understood as a child . . .

"Later on," Miss Hattie said as though she'd read Roxana's mind, "what Joss and Gideon Mapes will remember most about this terrible time is their wedding.''

"They have you to thank for that, and so do I. I don't know what we'd have done if we couldn't have come to you." Roxana hesitated and added shyly, "It makes me feel as though I've found an older sister, as well as a cousin."

Miss Hattie laughed and hugged her. "I have two older sisters and one younger one already, not to mention seven brothers! I'm sure I can make room for another!" She finished buttoning her nightgown, sat down on the edge of the bed, and looked at Roxana. "It's been very difficult for you, hasn't it, this trip? Much more than you've let show. I think your mother must be very proud of you."

She's used the present tense, Roxana thought dizzily, her eyes stinging. And suddenly, as at that moment back at Grey's Landing, her mother's presence seemed to be all around her. Distantly she heard Miss Hattie say gently, "I've always thought my mother has been like a guardian angel watching over me."

Roxana nodded, without speaking. "I'm glad I have your mother's name, Miss Hattie . . . I mean Mrs. Stowe."

Miss Hattie chuckled. "Sometimes, especially with Professor Stowe away, I have a hard time remembering my new identity myself!"

But before long you'll have the baby to remind you, Roxana thought. She asked shyly, "Did you really mean it when you said the best wish you could give Joss and Mr. Mapes is that they be as happy as you and Professor Stowe?"

"Oh, my dear, yes! Except their freedom, of course, and God and their friends will bring them that. It was very brave, and brilliant, of you to think of this masquerade by river, Roxana. It can't have been easy for you—in any sense."

Roxana suddenly found herself blushing, and turned away.

Behind her she heard Miss Hattie's voice, tender and amused, say, *"Yes??"* But nothing more was said until they were in bed with the lamp extinguished. Then somehow the whole story of the trip was spilling out.

"I was scared," Roxana confessed, and Miss Hattie answered calmly, "Of course. But you didn't let it show, or stop you."

"I daren't." Roxana paused. "It was scary, but it was exciting," she confessed. "I mean, I *knew* I could shoot. And I just couldn't believe God would let anything happen to Joss. Even the river . . . I couldn't believe it, but once the boat was moving, I wasn't *afraid* anymore . . . at least not of the water."

And then, inevitably and with an odd relief, she found herself telling Miss Hattie about Carlton Tanner. "He was so kind . . . I was so afraid he'd see through me, but he didn't." She heard Miss Hattie make a small sound that sounded remarkably like Joss's "mmm-*hmmm*." "I didn't know how to act . . . or why I felt afraid. The worst is, I don't know whether I was feeling that way because of the way he spoke of Joss and Gideon, or . . . something else."

There was a silence.

"Mr. Tanner," Miss Hattie said at last, "must be one of those men who have the terrible gift of intimacy. Not many do, I think. Brother Henry does, as I think you've noticed. It's a . . . I don't know; a way of looking into a woman's eyes, and smiling, that makes her believe there's some secret only they two share. A kind of spiritual oneness. It *is* a gift, and can be a great blessing if used wisely. My father has it; it's what makes him a great preacher. Mr. Stowe tells me I have it in my writing. My mother had it, and from what I understand, yours did too. And I do believe Mr. and Mrs. Mapes will share it."

"You said 'terrible,'" Roxana said in a small voice.

"It's only terrible when the person having it doesn't

understand its power, or the responsibility it entails. Used heedlessly or unwisely, it can leave a path of destruction in its wake."

The image of Carlton Tanner's face suddenly blazed behind Roxana's eyes. She actually felt breathless, and her heart was pounding, as it had when he kissed her wrist. And then, strangely, she found herself thinking, *But I unnerved him, too; I know I did. Is that why sometimes he behaved so brusquely?*

From the pillow next to hers she heard Miss Hattie's voice murmur, "Perhaps it's just as well you won't be seeing that young gentleman again. Fourteen's a bit young, even if your Mama did fall in love when she was that age."

Sunday was peaceful, a day of rest. All too soon it was Monday; time to take to the river again. It was hard taking leave of the Beechers; hard resuming the roles of "Miss Darden" and her slaves. Seeing Joss in her servant clothes, after her radiance in her wedding finery, made Roxana's heart ache. But Joss's eyes were serene. She was now Mrs. Gideon Mapes in the eyes of God and the State of Ohio. Things were going to be all right. The Beecher clan had said so. They had equipped both Joss and Roxana with the names and addresses of Anti-Slavery people they were to seek out on the rest of the journey.

"Good-bye, little sister," Miss Hattie said, hugging Roxana. "Write and tell me how the journey goes."

"Write and tell me about the baby." Roxana hugged her back, carefully. "Thank you *so* much. I love you." She couldn't say good-bye.

Golden Lad lifted his muzzle and keened in sympathy, and Miss Hattie scratched his ear. "We're going to miss you, too," she assured him.

Uncle Sam Foote drove them to the dock. He had many

business interests throughout the city, Henry Ward said. No one would think it strange he drove "Miss Darden" and her slaves to the pier. The boat was already being loaded with cargo when they arrived. Golden Lad jumped down eagerly, and Gideon had difficulty holding him.

The *Allegheny Belle* was newer and grander than the *Maria Q.* Her crew were nattily uniformed and polite, and made no objection to Miss Darden requiring her servants close at hand. Twin flights of steps swept in curves up to the Boiler Deck. Gideon took the trunk to the good-sized stateroom, then disappeared, coming back up later to report that he'd been able to stake a claim to some comfortable-looking bales right beneath Roxana's window. He took Golden Lad off to make friends on the Main Deck.

Roxana and Joss unpacked. Joss smoothed the white silk mull gently as she shook it out, her eyes dreamy. "I meant it when I said it's yours," Roxana reminded.

Joss shook her head. "It's not right. Anyway, I'll have no place to wear it."

"It *is* right. Mama would say so," Roxana insisted, not realizing till the words were out that she was speaking of her mother without sorrow. So hurt did fade, as Miss Hattie had said. "You'll wear it in Canada. Or put it away to save with the rose petals from your bouquet. I saw you press them." Roxana looked around. "I wonder how soon we'll start."

"We left the pier fifteen minutes ago. Didn't you notice?" Joss asked, amused.

Roxana stared at her, then out the window. Sure enough, the scenery was slipping by. *And I wasn't afraid,* Roxana thought. *I wasn't thinking about it, and I wasn't afraid.*

. . . I put away childish things . . .

No, her fears hadn't been childish. But they had been torment, as the Bible said.

That evening she donned one of her mother's dinner gowns and went to the dining table with the other passengers. Her fear of not carrying off the masquerade was gone. If she could fool Henry Ward Beecher, she could fool anyone, couldn't she?

Aboard the *Allegheny Belle,* dinner was the evening meal. The food was considerably better than on the *Maria Q.* Turtle soup, then a choice of three sorts of fish, then the meats: chicken, turkey, beef, lamb, and ham, each available boiled or roasted or turned into fancy "made dishes" like pies or cutlets or patties with French names. Rice, three kinds of potatoes, eighteen kinds of vegetables. Seventeen different desserts, including both almond and cranberry tarts and the very elegant and hard to come by ice cream and sherbet. And then, rounding off the meal, fruits and nuts and coffee. Roxana had never drunk coffee, but guessed that "Miss Darden" would. It was very bitter, but drinkable after she added a lot of cream and three spoons of sugar.

Later, after smuggling food back to the stateroom for Joss and Gideon, Roxana went back to the Ladies' Saloon. Just beyond drawn-back draperies of goffered velvet, a man with oiled black hair played piano in the Main Saloon. After a while the center space became a dance floor. Roxana watched eagerly, trying to remember the steps her mother had taught her as a child. Mama danced like a leaf in the breeze, she thought, and for the first time the memory of it was not painful.

As before, Joss slept in the stateroom with Roxana,

though she was no longer shy about spending the evening down on the Main Deck. She was asleep in the upper bunk when Roxana awoke on Tuesday morning, although Roxana had no recollection of her coming in. Breakfast, too, was better than it had been on the *Maria Q*, and the midday meal was a cold buffet. Two elderly ladies who had sat near Roxana at the dinner table invited her to join them on the upper deck's shady side. A ship's steward carried their plates out for them and drew small tables up beside their chairs.

At first Roxana assumed her Aunt Darden manner, but soon found that she could—almost—be herself. "To Pittsburgh," she answered, when asked how far she was traveling, and "visiting friends" when asked where she'd been.

"And you're traveling alone?" Mrs. Raeburn asked.

"I have my maid along, and a bodyguard," Roxana replied. "I had kin with me in Cincinnati." That was true in a way these southern ladies would never imagine, she thought, and added, "I'm hoping my father will join me," which was definitely true.

"And will your mother be joining you also?" Miss Hannaford inquired.

"My mother is dead."

She tried to say it simply, but it didn't work too well. One of the ladies said, "Oh, I'm so sorry," and the other, "We've been tactless. Please forgive us."

"It's quite all right," Roxana murmured, and was surprised to find that that was true. She *wasn't* reacting as she would have weeks before. And then her attention—everyone's attention—was distracted. A golden streak, large and friendly and trailing a green leash, launched himself at Roxana and covered her with kisses.

"*Down*, boy!" Roxana cried instinctively.

"Ah'm so sorry, Miss Zan. Ah thought you'd want to see him, an' he got away." Joss, alarmed, came running to catch at Golden Lad's leash.

"It's all right. I'll walk him around the deck a bit. You may go back down," Roxana said meaningfully, catching Joss's eye.

"Yes, ma'am. Thank you, ma'am." Joss curtsied and escaped.

Golden Lad, suddenly the gentleman, sat down, offered everyone his paw, and then curled himself under Roxana's chair.

"Handsome animal," Miss Hannaford said.

"Nice girl you have," Mrs. Raeburn remarked. "Has she been in your family long?"

"Yes, she has."

The conversation dwindled into a discussion of the servant problem between Mrs. Raeburn and her sister. After a while Roxana was able to leave.

But it went all right, she thought. *I'm learning to be a lady grown. They accepted me as what I said I was. Even Golden Lad behaved—almost.*

That evening there was a concert in the main saloon and, again, dancing. Roxana watched the lines of ladies and of gentlemen advance towards each other, bow or curtsey, then move back; advance again so that each gentleman's gloved hand took a lady's, also gloved. Arms lifted high, they revolved around each other, retreated, bowed or curtsied. Then the lines split into eight couples, then four, then two, then one. *Down* the length of the Main Saloon; separate into the lines again; *up* around the outside, then duck down and go in couples beneath the arch made by the lead couple's raised arms. . . . Beneath her concealing skirts, Roxana's toes tapped to the tune.

"Do you not dance, Miss Darden?" Miss Hannaford asked over lunch on the gallery the next day.

"Hush, sister, perhaps she has religious scruples," Mrs. Raeburn reproved.

Roxana smiled at Miss Hannaford. "I'm Episcopalian, and I was taught dancing when I was young. But I've never danced in a public place." She looked at Mrs. Raeburn. "Would it be proper?"

The sisters conferred. "Traveling in the upper class on shipboard is rather regarded as an introduction, as if one were attending a large private party. Since you are old enough to have had an 'understanding,' with your father's blessing"—the fib about her recovering from the death of a sweetheart had been resurrected—"if a gentleman of the right sort invites you to dance, I can see no harm in your accepting," Mrs. Raeburn pronounced.

"It would make your solitary journey more enjoyable," her sister added. Traveling with servants did not count as traveling with companions.

Not that anyone's likely to invite me to dance anyway, Roxana thought. But the possibility was enticing.

By dinnertime that evening, though, the strains of the past weeks caught up. Roxana could barely keep her eyes open through dinner, and went gratefully back to her stateroom where Golden Lad was waiting. Travel on the *Allegheny Belle* was so smooth she was barely conscious of being on the water. She heard the sounds of banjo, harmonica, and singing drifting up from the Main Deck, and hoped Joss and Gideon were having a good time. *If only Joss could dress up pretty and have a real wedding journey*, she thought. But of course Joss dared not risk it.

The next day was much as the ones before, although the sky was overcast. They were traveling up-river ahead of a rainstorm, Joss reported. The ship's pilot was trying to outrace it. He had ordered the crew to keep the boiler fully stoked at all times. They had taken on a great deal of lumber during a nighttime stop, far more than usual, so the *Allegheny Belle* now sat lower on the water. The pilot, not the captain, was the true ruler of the steamboat. The captain was owner, or part owner, responsible for the business end of things and for the comfort of Boiler Deck passengers. The engineer reigned in the boiler room. Joss was learning a great deal during her visits to the Main Deck.

She came back each night to sleep in the bunk above Roxana's, and she took Golden Lad down to the Main Deck with her for exercise and training, and to keep him out of trouble. That afternoon she brought Golden Lad to where Roxana sat with Mrs. Raeburn and her sister, who had apparently appointed themselves her chaperones. "De Main Deck very crowded, Miz Darden, an' engineer say he best be kep' up here. Afternoon, ma'am, ma'am," Joss added, curtseying to the women.

"A nice girl, that," Mrs. Raeburn said approvingly when Joss was gone. "You wouldn't want to part with her, I suppose? I'd pay you a good price."

"Goodness, no!" Roxana exclaimed, shocked.

Golden Lad sat down, lifted his muzzle skyward and keened.

"Storm coming," Mrs. Raeburn said, and began gathering up her belongings. A few slanting raindrops hit the deck, and she rose. "Come along, sister." They made their way inside. The deck quickly emptied. Roxana remained, reveling in the cool, damp air. Miss Hattie was right, things do change, she thought. She was hardly afraid of the river anymore.

The rain beat down harder. Golden Lad rose on his hind

legs, rested his elbows on the railing, and looked overboard with interest. Roxana jerked his leash. "Come on, you clown, let's take a walk." *All we need*, she thought, *is for him to take a dive!*

By keeping close to the inner walls it was possible to walk around the deck without getting pelted with rain. But the deck was slippery. Fortunately, there were railings along the walls, and she held on. Golden Lad, happily slithering, plunged ahead.

Without warning, the leash was jerked out of Roxana's hand.

Drat that dog! Roxana thought. He was already far ahead and, turning the corner of the prow, he disappeared from sight.

By the time she reached the corner and emerged onto open deck, the rain was beating hard. Her broad-brimmed hat flapped wetly in the wind. Her hair was falling down across her face, and she dashed it back, blinking raindrops from her eyes.

A laughing voice said, "We've met like this before, I believe."

Carlton Tanner. Carlton, tipping his hat with one gloved hand and with the other holding tight to a familiar bottle-green leash. Golden Lad sat wagging his tail, looking half exultant and half ashamed.

"Where did you come from?" Roxana exclaimed, startled. Taking that as his cue, Golden Lad reared up and hugged her. Carlton Tanner laughed.

"I haven't seen *you* till now, either," he retorted. "Where have *you* been keeping yourself?"

But he hasn't answered my question, Roxana thought. He knows we've both been ashore; this is the *Allegheny Belle*, not the *Maria Q*. Two could play this game, she thought.

"I've been visiting friends. What were you doing while you were ashore?"

"Taking care of some business for my father," he said easily. "Shall we go inside and have some tea? That nigra girl of yours can take care of Boy."

"I really prefer to look after him myself. He may have caught a chill. Thank you so much," Roxana said, politely taking back the leash. Carlton Tanner, his eyes quizzical, backed off and bowed.

Golden Lad, the perfect gentleman also, trotted obediently at Roxana's side as she went through the Ladies' Saloon, annoyed at feeling flustered. She dragged him into the stateroom, which was empty. Joss must still be below. *I hope she's not getting soaked*, Roxana thought, and then, *but that's Gideon's responsibility now, isn't it?*

Another few days, and I won't be Joss's responsibility anymore, either.

Don't think about that. Think about how wonderful it is that they're married and will be free. Think about getting Golden Lad dry, not to mention quiet. He was in the mood for keening again. Roxana rubbed him vigorously with a towel, then dried herself.

She managed to dress for dinner, without help, in one of her mother's dinner gowns. The neck, low for Roxana, almost dropped off the shoulders and was finished with a fall of fine old lace. Roxana did her own hair and was proud of the result. Decidedly, she looked older, and no longer felt uncomfortable pretending that she was.

She waited until nearly everyone was at table before slipping out of the stateroom and into the chair that Mrs. Raeburn and her sister had kept for her. Carlton Tanner was at the far end, near the Gents' Bar, by the captain.

After dinner, there again was music. A lady sang a song

in German, with many trills that made her three chins quiver. Roxana, irresistibly reminded of Golden Lad, had difficulty keeping from smiling. Involuntarily, she found herself looking down the table to where Carlton Tanner's eyes twinkled at her as though he'd read her mind.

Later, when there was a break in the music, he approached. "The resemblance is remarkable, isn't it?" he murmured.

Roxana snapped her fan open. "I don't know what you mean."

"Yes, you do." The music began again, and couples were taking places for dancing. Carlton Tanner bowed and held out his gloved hand. "May I have the honor, Miss Darden?"

Roxana hesitated. Mrs. Raeburn and her sister were far to one side, not close enough to consult. They had said dancing with a proper gentleman would be all right, hadn't they? Roxana, her heart pounding, placed her gloved hand in his and let him lead her to the floor.

She *did* remember the steps. And it *was* splendid. They danced three sets, and by then the air in the room was thick with lamp smoke. Roxana fanned herself.

"You are tired. Shall I take you to your seat? Or perhaps a breath of air." Before she knew what was happening Carlton Tanner guided her out onto the deck. The rain had all but ceased, and a moon was riding through scudding clouds.

Roxana took a deep breath. "You were right. It is better out here."

"Shall we take a stroll?" Carlton Tanner tucked her arm through his and started off without waiting for her response. Suddenly Roxana felt a quite real chill.

"I think I'd best go in," she said, stopping still.

"I'll see you to your door."

"No—please. I'll be quite all right. Thank you."

"As you wish." At the door to the Ladies' Saloon Carlton Tanner stopped, bowed, and before opening the door lifted her right hand, turned it over, and kissed the small opening below the glove button where her skin showed through.

Roxana snatched her hand away and went through the doorway, scarcely aware he was holding the door open.

THIRTEEN

"**I** don't think I'll go out to breakfast," Roxana said next morning. "Get something sent in for me, will you? I mean for us."

"Baby, what's wrong?" Joss came over quickly. "You're not coming down with something, are you?" She felt Roxana's forehead. "No fever. Did you get wet in the rain?"

"I just don't feel like getting up," Roxana said, avoiding the last question.

"That does not sound like you. Leastwise, not since we got to Cincinnati." Joss looked her straight in the eye. "Talk to me, Zan."

Roxana stirred uncomfortably. "Carlton Tanner's on board. Golden Lad got away from me on deck again, and he returned him, just as before."

"Mmm-*hmmm.*" Joss waited.

"He asked me to dance last night. And I did."

"You *what?*" Joss exclaimed, her eyes darkening.

"The ladies said it would be all right," Roxana said de-

148

fensively. Joss knew all about Mrs. Raeburn and Miss Hannaford.

"And just when did they tell you that? And why?"

"Because they were wondering yesterday why I hadn't danced the night before. I asked if that would be proper, and they said it would."

"For age twenty, yes. For eighteen, maybe. You're not eighteen."

"I can't have them thinking I'm not, can I? Anyway," Roxana concluded, "I'm not planning to dance again." She didn't say why, and she didn't tell Joss about the kiss on the hand. Or what Miss Hattie had said about the "terrible gift of intimacy."

Joss looked at her shrewdly but said no more. She fetched breakfast, and Joss and Roxana ate, and then Joss took the remainder down to Gideon and stayed below. Roxana stayed in the stateroom and tried to read. Her mind, and her stomach, were whirling. Beyond the window the sky was that odd yellow gray, and people, buildings and animals along the shore seemed like figures in faded old paintings. When she emerged from the stateroom for lunch she found the buffet line half deserted and most of the passengers sitting inside. To her relief, Carlton Tanner was nowhere in sight. She spotted the ladies and went to join them, but even they seemed subdued.

"You weren't at breakfast," Mrs. Raeburn said, half statement, half question.

"I had a headache." That was only half a lie. "It was the weather," Roxana added. "I'm much better now." She saw the women exchange glances, but they said nothing more. A waiter came by, offering tea. Roxana sipped hers gratefully.

"*There* you are." Carlton Tanner stopped beside her

chair. He bowed courteously to the women and turned to Roxana. "I was concerned when I did not see you on deck this morning. If you would like me to exercise Boy for you, I shall be pleased to do so. You can send your girl to find me. Ladies." He bowed again and strode away.

"I'm sorry," Roxana murmured, embarrassed. "I meant to introduce you."

"It's quite all right," Miss Hannaford said hurriedly. "Isn't it, sister?"

Mrs. Raeburn, for the first time in the journey, looked undecided.

"Is anything wrong?" Roxana asked quickly.

Mrs. Raeburn hesitated and then, abruptly, spoke in a low hurried tone. "My dear, please forgive an old woman, but I really must speak plainly. It was very unwise of you to dance with that young person."

"Wh—" Roxana straightened, stared, and felt her face flame. "But you said it would be all right for me to accept a gentleman's invitation to dance!"

"A proper gentleman, I said. Which, forgive me, that fellow is not. Surely you could see—"

Roxana's heart was pounding and her whole body burned as it had when he had kissed her palm. "Mr. Carlton Tanner," she said, enunciating carefully, "*is* a gentleman. Why, he—"

"Is that what he's calling himself?" Mrs. Raeburn glanced at her sister, who tittered and hurriedly covered her mouth with her hand. "Gentlemanly, yes, but scarcely a gentleman." Her voice softened. "I'd forgotten that your mother is dead, and of course you've had no occasion to encounter . . . Miss Darden, I'm sorry to shock you, but the fellow—whoever he is, he was not calling himself Tanner when we first encountered him—is a common bounty hunter. That's the 'business' he travels on for his father.''

Roxana stared, her mouth going dry.

"They're both slave agents,'' Mrs. Raeburn said bluntly. "Seeking and returning runaways to their owners, and doing the occasional trade. A dreadful business, but necessary in these unsettled times. Someone has to do it, of course, but one scarcely has to *receive* these people socially—Miss Darden, are you ill?''

"Excuse me.'' Roxana clapped her hand over her face and stumbled to her feet, shaking off the ladies' offers to accompany her to the stateroom. The door key shook in her hand. At last the key turned in the lock; she was inside, the door locked behind her; she was leaning against it, her body shaking with the dry heaves.

It would be a relief if she could be sick; if she could blot out the whole past twenty-four hours . . . no, both boat trips, entirely . . . but she could not. She pulled off her outer clothes and corset, put on her wrapper, and threw herself on the bunk.

Gentlemanly, yes, but scarcely a gentleman . . . Why had she assumed that slave agents naturally looked like monsters? *Someone has to do it* . . .

But not him, her heart cried out, and her mind answered inexorably, *What made you sure he was a true gentleman? When you know what even your own uncle was like? What did you know of him, other than that he's handsome, dresses well, and is attracted to you?*

If he is attracted, and not just spying on Joss and Gideon . . .

Joss and Gideon.

You <u>didn't</u> *trust him,* the voice in her head said. *You know you didn't, not deep down. You liked the attention. You danced with him. You let him kiss your hand.*

The door creaked, and then Joss was there. "Mrs. Raeburn found me. She was worried about you. Are you ill?"

"He's a slave catcher," Roxana said baldly.

"Who?" Joss sank down as if her legs had given out under her.

"Carlton Tanner. And no, I didn't do anything to give you away. He doesn't know. Any more than I knew—" Roxana sat up, her hands across her face. "I haven't given anything away, I swear," she repeated. "But I danced with him. I let him get close to me."

The terrible gift of intimacy, Miss Hattie had said. She started to shake again.

"Baby, baby." Joss was rocking her, smoothing her hair. "You weren't to know. You're only fourteen."

"All I was trying to do was convince folks I was older. For a good cause. Now look what it's done—"

"Zan, stop it!" Joss seized her hands and pulled them down. "You did what you had to do to keep up the masquerade. It troubles my conscience that I got you into it."

"It was my idea—"

"And I went along with it. I promised your father I'd look after you—"

"I guess there's enough blame to go around," Roxana said tiredly. "One thing's sure. I'm never going near Mr. Carlton Tanner again. I couldn't."

"Yes, you can. You must. You can't give him reason to suspect you're not what you seem, either. You'll have to just . . . treat him with more reserve. And no more dancing," Joss finished sternly.

Roxana nodded. "I couldn't. Not ever." She never wanted him to touch her again.

Somehow, she managed to make herself presentable for dinner. She reassumed the Aunt Darden manner, and went to her place between the elderly sisters at table at the last moment, and thanked them for their kind warning. With them, at least, nothing more need be said, and they both were comforting and maternal.

She battled against the impulse to look down the table to where Carlton Tanner sat talking easily with the captain and other important-looking men. Men with whom he did business? She didn't want to know.

She longed to flee the saloons after dinner, but it seemed necessary to follow her usual routine. So she sat between her two elderly guardians, and when Carlton Tanner came to ask her to dance it was Mrs. Raeburn who answered, "Miss Darden is not dancing this evening," in a tone that would have frozen the Sahara. She kept her eyes on her lap, and listened to his footsteps recede. Presently she saw him dancing with an older woman.

"I think it will be safe now for you to slip away," Mrs. Raeburn said gently.

"Yes . . . thank you. More than I can say." Impulsively, Roxana bent and kissed each woman's cheek. They might be slave owners, but they were kind.

She made her way to the side of the Ladies' Saloon and then, after hesitating, slipped outside. It was safe, because *he* was dancing, and she needed air. The whole ship was suffocatingly hot. The pilot was, apparently, still racing the storm. On deck the vibrations and heat from the boiler were even more noticeable. *How can Joss and Gideon stand it down there?* she wondered idly. *Because they have to,* the voice in her head answered mockingly.

If only rain would come and cool the air! If only *he'd* leave the ship at its next stop.

A breeze sprang up, and she walked into it, the slap of the damp air a comfort against her face. She walked mechanically, clear around the boat, past the great wheel turning, until she was back outside the window of her own stateroom. She could hear Golden Lad keening inside, his whimpering escalating into piercing cries.

When someone touched her hand she almost screamed.

"Hush! Don't! It's only I. We don't want to draw those fire-breathing gorgons, do we?" Carlton Tanner's voice was warm and teasing, as though nothing at all were wrong.

"Go away."

"What's wrong?" His head bent closer, and she could smell the scent of tobacco and the bay rum gentlemen used to sleek their hair. Roxana almost gagged. But she mustn't. She must stand straight and tall, and keep moving. Except she couldn't move, because he was standing so that he'd pinned her against the rail.

"If you don't let me go I'll scream," Roxana hissed between gritted teeth.

"I mean you no harm. Just tell me how I've offended you, and I'll leave. Is it because I kissed your hand? Surely suitors have dared that before!"

"It's not that!" Roxana straightened, and something in her eyes must have reached him, because he stepped back slightly. Not enough for her to get past, but enough so she could look him in the eyes. And she did. "You're a slave hunter!"

"Is that all?" To her astonishment and revulsion, he laughed. "My dear, is that all?" It was the laugh that made her realize, suddenly and sharply, that she'd been hoping he'd deny it. But he didn't. He didn't think it needed to be denied.

"You are, aren't you?" she heard herself saying in a tone of childlike surprise.

"I told you I was a business agent. You never asked in what business," Carlton Tanner said reasonably. "I suppose to a lady as fastidious as you"—was there a trace of scorn in his tone?—"being in trade makes me somehow less worthy. But it's honest, necessary work, and I do it well."

"It's not the being in trade! It's what the trade is! Human beings—"

"Oh, come now," Carlton Tanner drawled, and she wondered how she'd ever found his voice entrancing. She drew a ragged breath, realizing vaguely that she had suddenly grown very hot, that the ship was vibrating even worse than before. She heard his voice as from a great distance. "Scarcely human as you or I know that term. Two or three generations removed from the jungle? I admit some are bright, but you can't get round the basic fact. Slaves are *property.*"

Roxana's hand came up and struck him, hard, across the face.

At that same moment, like a crescendo from a giant drum, came a great crash, and a rush of steam, and suddenly wood and metal were flying through the air.

"BOILER'S EXPLODED!" Carlton Tanner swept his arm around her as the deck pitched suddenly sidewards. "Can you swim?" his voice came urgently in her ear. Roxana nodded. Then she screamed, as in one swift gesture he swept her up and threw her over the rail.

She landed in the water, went under, and came up gasping.

Three feet away, the *Allegheny Belle* listed dangerously. Flames and a cloud of foul dark smoke shot upwards. She saw Carlton Tanner, still on board, dive off and surface near her. He grabbed her arm and began swimming with her towards shore. She gasped and struggled. "Stop!" he ordered. "I can't get you away if you struggle. The whole thing's going down, and there'll be a suction—"

Screams and cries were coming from the ship, where figures moved frantically, silhouetted against the flames. Over Carlton Tanner's shoulder she saw Gideon's great bulk lift Joss and toss her over the rail.

Roxana beat against Carlton Tanner's chest. *"Joss!"*

"Don't look," he ordered roughly. "You can buy another girl—"

"She's my cousin, damn you!"

She heard him catch his breath. For a brief instant his grip relaxed, and she jerked herself free. With a muttered oath, Carlton Tanner grabbed a passing plank and thrust it at her. "Hang onto this and kick like hell towards shore!" he ordered. Then he struck out, with an experienced swimmer's stroke, back towards the burning ship.

The cries of passengers were in the air. She couldn't see Joss, though her eyes searched frantically through the darkness. She did see Gideon jump overboard and head towards shore with giant strokes. There was another explosion, and flames shooting upwards, and then the whirlpool suction Carlton Tanner had spoken of occurred. The waters opened, and swirled, like a mighty funnel, pulling down into its depth the entire ship and scattering bodies and body parts in all directions.

FOURTEEN

Waves of foul water leaped shoreward from the drowning ship, engulfing floating debris and struggling humans. Their force pulled Roxana under and tore the wooden plank out of her grip. She was sucked down, as water choked her screams.

Don't panic, a voice in her head, that could have been her mother's voice, said quietly. *You know how to swim—*

Somehow her flailings became sure swimmer's movements. She shot upward, and trod water. She was afraid to head for shore, for the waters surged like a whirlpool, full of hidden dangers, and her garments dragged her down. She stared towards the inferno that had been the *Allegheny Queen,* blinking water out of her eyes, too numb to even pray.

She could see nothing clearly. No sign of Joss, who could have been sucked downward in the explosion. No sign of Gideon . . . *If he hadn't been African, he wouldn't have been trapped on the Main Deck when fire broke out. If*

Joss hadn't loved him, she wouldn't have been down there with him. She, Roxana, up with the rich white folks on the upper level, had been able to jump clear. *Not jump; been thrown, as Joss had been thrown, but further, sooner . . . and by a slavecatcher. A slavecatcher who had gone back for Joss because of her. . . .*

Something grabbed Roxana's sleeve.

She struggled, fighting, and then a familiar sharp grip closed around her arm. *Golden Lad.* Golden Lad, swimming happily, pulling and pushing her towards the nearest shore.

"You big beautiful clown," Roxana gasped, her eyes filling with tears. She felt for his leash, but he wore none . . . *thank goodness; no danger of its getting caught on a snag* . . . and locked the fingers of her left hand tightly around his collar. She tried to swim, to help, but something inexorable made her turn her head towards where the ship had been . . . where what was left of it still was, jackknifed and burning against the midnight sky. Each time she stopped to look, Golden Lad nudged her back towards the shoreline until, at last, she felt arms reach down and haul her up the bank. Hands released her onto dry ground. Golden Lad stood over her and licked her face.

"Smart dog, that," a man's voice said. Roxana nodded, too weak to speak. "Someone will look after you soon," the voice added, fading away. She lay there, retching, and Golden Lad lay beside her. Occasionally he lifted his head and whined.

"Find Joss . . . try to find Joss," she whispered, but Golden Lad would not budge. After awhile men's voices approached again. A blanket was wrapped around her. Then someone was lifting her, carrying her to a wagon, trying to prevent Golden Lad from following and finally giving up. Roxana lay in the wagon bed, vaguely aware of others around her. Golden Lad sat beside her and keened. Footsteps and men's voices came and went. . . . Each time, as another victim was laid in the wagon, she struggled to ask about Joss, about Gideon, and each time no one paid her any heed.

Finally the wagon clattered off, up a steep trace along the riverbank. It stopped before a large brick building where lamps burned in windows and lanterns hung beside the open doors. Gilt letters on the glass above them glinted the word HOTEL. Arms reached out again to lift her.

Afterwards, Roxana remembered saying distinctly, "I can walk," and being allowed to try. Raindrops felt like tears against her face. After a few steps she stumbled, and was carried inside. She remembered crying out "JOSS!" but that was all.

The next thing Roxana knew she was looking upwards at flames burning in a bright brass chandelier.

She struggled to sit up, and a woman's voice said, "I wouldn't, there's a love. Best lie still till you're feeling better."

"I can't! I have to find . . . !"

"Whoever they are, they'll be brought here if they escaped," the woman said. She was kind and motherly looking. "Leastwise, if they escaped towards the Ohio shore they'll be here. Those that jumped from the other side of the boat are in Kentucky. The menfolk will sort it all out in the morning, don't you worry."

"My dog . . ."

The woman chuckled. "He's right beside you."

Roxana's groping fingers found a familiar silken coat, its waves now matted. A rough tongue began busily to lick her face, and she sputtered. "Stop that, you idiot!"

"He's no idiot," the woman said, amused. "You could

both use a heap of washing, but that'll have to wait. . . . Ah, Doctor! Here's a young lady for you to check over."

A big man with a harassed, anxious face bent over her; had her move her head, her arms, and what he delicately referred to as her "limbs." "No wounds or broken bones," he pronounced. "Just you lie here, miss, till someone can find a room for you for the night. If not here, in one of the other hotels. I'll look you over again in the morning."

"Where am I?" Roxana thought to ask.

"Marietta, Ohio." The doctor moved away.

"Wait! Please!" Roxana struggled up. "My—my servants—" Just in time, she'd remembered there was still need for the masquerade.

"They'll be out back in the stables, along with any ship's laborers who escaped, poor brutes. Mrs. Anderson, I need your help with the seriously injured." The two went away.

Roxana sat up, locked her arms around her knees, and looked around.

She was in a long room that was probably a ballroom. The chandelier flames were reflected in stylish tall mirrors around the walls, hanging at intervals between mural panels of a river scene. Trees, and riverbanks, and a small, brown boy fishing . . . a couple that reminded her of her father and mother, strolling along a bluff . . . children playing . . . a steamboat puffing along the river, being hailed by two Africans on a passing raft. Furniture lined the walls, delicate settees and chairs covered in fine brocade.

Golden Lad sat up and keened.

"Go look for them, boy," Roxana murmured in his ear. "Joss and Gideon—and Mr. Tanner."

Golden Lad trotted off around the room, his tail a wet banner. She saw him sniffing people, and occasionally being patted, but presently he trotted back and stood foursquare before her. He had found no one.

I must go to the stables, Roxana thought, and realized she was holding back. She hauled herself to her feet, using Golden Lad for leverage. Her whole body ached. And she was shivering. She found the blanket she'd been lying in, and wrapped it around herself. Then, followed by Golden Lad, she picked her way around the room's perimeter towards a door at the far end. It would probably open near the stables—

She was almost to the door when she heard it, dark-toned and beautiful and reassuring.

Deep river,
My home is over Jordan . . .

Joss was out there. Joss was alive. Roxana almost ran across the rain-soaked back yard of the hotel and found her way blocked at the stable door.

"You can't go in there, miss. T'aint fittin'."

"I must! Joss—my servants are in there, and I have to see—"

"T'ain't fittin'," the man repeated inexorably, and reached to move her.

Growling low in his throat, Golden Lad reared on his hind legs and knocked the man aside. Roxana darted in, and Golden Lad followed, his neck hairs bristling. The stable was thick with darkness. Two lanterns burned, revealing figures lying or sitting everywhere. There was no room to walk between them. To her shame, she was suddenly and deeply afraid.

Far off in the inner reaches of the stables, the familiar voice went on.

De-e-ep river, Lord . . .

Roxana did the only thing she could think of. She wet her lips and answered.

I want to cross over into campground, Lord!

There was a muffled cry within the crowded darkness, and then Golden Lad plunged in, galloping over lying figures to meet Joss as she ran forward.

"Baby, baby," Joss crooned, hugging Roxana. "Sweet Jesus, thank You! I was afraid to die and face her mama . . ."

"Gideon?" Roxana blurted, afraid of what she might hear. But Joss's face was serene.

"He's in there. He's been burned some, and his leg's broken, but the doctor's set it." Joss's voice cracked. "Gideon almost didn't make it off the boat because he was helping the stokers try to prevent the fire from spreading."

"Joss, I'm so sorry. . . . If I hadn't thought up this river trip—"

"*Zan, stop it!* If you hadn't—you know what, if you hadn't," Joss said sternly. Then her face softened. "He's a good man, that doctor. He says Gideon will be fine." She held Roxana off and looked at her closely. "What about you?"

"I'm fine, too. Leastwise, in body. And you can see how Golden Lad is." Roxana, for the first time, began to really see around her, and what she saw made her giddy relief fade quickly. "It's really bad, isn't it?" she whispered.

Joss nodded. "Those poor souls on the Main Deck, especially the roustabouts . . . but 'most all the men, even those who'd been likkered up, pitched in to keep the boat running. Some of the women, too. And after the explosion, helping people . . . So many were lost, Zan. From where Gideon was, he could see . . . And so many badly hurt and needing nursing. I've been trying to help. . . ."

"I will, too." Roxana took a step forward, was met again by the white man who'd stopped her earlier.

"Can't allow you to go in with those people, miss!"

Golden Lad growled deep in his throat. Joss looked at the man coldly. "My mistress wishes to help with the nursing. Her father's a very important man in this state. In this country! I wouldn't want to be in your shoes if you lay a finger on her."

The man backed off.

The night passed in a haze of smoke and smells and the moans of dying men. The dead were instantly carried to one side and stacked like cordwood with those already there. There were women's bodies in the pile, too, and smaller figures. . . . "Are all the bodies here?" Roxana asked at one point.

Joss shook her head. "Boiler Deck passengers are in the hotel. In the kitchen, I think."

"How do people know—"

"They're sorted out by clothing, and the color of their skin."

Even in death, Roxana thought.

With the soot and oil, how can anyone tell the color of skin? Joss's color could be that of either race.

Roxana felt as though she was on the brink of some important thought, but her brain was too weary. So were her legs. She tried to rise from the floor, to move from one badly burned figure to another, and found her knees buckling.

The man from the door was back, and now respectful. "A room's been found for you in the hotel, miss—"

"Darden," Joss supplied evenly. "Miss Darden will be right along."

"I can't—" Roxana started to say, then stopped. "I shall come directly, and my maid here and her husband will come with me. She will show you where her husband is. His leg's broken; he must be transported on a pallet. I shall wait here while you do so." She drew herself to her full height and stared the man directly in the eye.

To her astonishment and relief, she was obeyed.

They found themselves in a suite of rooms, bedroom and sitting room, elegant with mahogany and honey-blonde polished furniture. The men, stone-faced, laid Gideon's pallet on the floor of the sitting-room and left. Roxana locked the door behind them firmly.

Gideon, despite his wounds, began to laugh. "I wish you could see the look on your face, Miss Grey!"

"Miss Darden. It's too soon yet to risk anything," Roxana cautioned.

"What do we do now?" Joss asked.

Outside the windows dawn was breaking. "We sleep," Roxana said wearily. "I'm too tired to think of anything yet."

There was a pitcher of steaming water on the washstand, and she and Joss managed to wash themselves. She slept in her chemise, which was dirty but dry, in the big bed, and Joss slept on the floor by Gideon's pallet in the sitting room.

Joss's warning to the man in the barn must have permeated to the furthest reaches of the hotel. In the morning, a large breakfast was delivered to the suite without being ordered.

"Beg pardon, Miss Darden, but how do you plan to pay for all this?" Gideon asked as Joss fed him fruit. She refused to allow him to sit up without a doctor's permission. "Everything you brought with you's gone down with the ship. The trunk may float to shore, but 'tisn't likely."

Roxana, back in the bedraggled dinner gown, blushed. She turned her back and reached down inside its neckline, between her breasts. She laid the items one by one on the table . . . the pearl-handled revolver, the thick packet of papers wrapped in oiled silk, the roll of money. "I've been afraid to leave them off my person at any time," she confessed. "They've been inside my—" She patted her corset. "And under my pillow all night. I'm afraid your freedom papers may have gotten soaked, Joss, but if we spread them out carefully perhaps they'll dry without the ink running."

Gideon looked from one of them to the other, dumbstruck, but Joss started to laugh. She, too, reached down her bodice and produced a roll of money. "I had the same thought! Our wedding present from the Greys," she said to Gideon. "I was afraid to tell you till we were heading North, for fear you'd think we shouldn't take it."

Gideon stared at her for a moment, then roared with laughter. "What a woman I've married! Resourceful in all emergencies. I wouldn't dream of telling you not to take anything given you, love. Put your mind instead to worrying about what we do next."

They were interrupted by a loud slurping. Golden Lad had found the milk pitcher and was helping himself.

Joss pulled herself to her feet. "I'd better take him for a walk before he disgraces himself on this fancy carpet. I'll look around town. Maybe there's a shop where we can buy some clothes. Or at least yard goods." She was an accomplished seamstress.

Before she could leave, a knock sounded at the door. They all froze.

"Who is it?" Roxana demanded in her most Aunt Darden-ish voice.

"Hotel manager. Gentleman here who demands to see Miss Darden."

Carlton Tanner. The thought flew into Roxana's mind on the instant, and at the same time, *I don't want to see him! I don't wish him dead, but I don't want to see him—*

She stared at Joss in panic, and at the same time a very familiar voice said firmly, "I'm sure Miss Darden will see me. You may leave."

Roxana rushed to the door, barely waiting till footsteps had receded before flinging it open and falling into her father's arms.

FIFTEEN

"The Beechers arranged for Zan's letter to me to be taken to Washington by special courier," Judge Grey explained. "Traveling straight through the nights, with changes of driver and horse. Mrs. Stowe's own letter went along, too, telling me everything, including the timetable of the *Allegheny Belle*. She's a very intelligent lady. And a very kind one."

"That's what I always told you," Roxana murmured.

"I took her suggestion and left for Ohio by the same means," Judge Grey went on, "meaning to board the *Allegheny Belle* in Marietta. You can imagine my horror when I reached here and heard what had happened!" He reached for Zan's hand and held it tightly.

"At least you remembered to ask for Miss Darden," Roxana said.

"I did. And don't think I didn't appreciate the irony."

It was several hours later, hours in which Judge Grey had, as Mam Lucy would say, "raised a deal of dust." The doctor had been persuaded that Gideon could be moved to a private home. Arrangements had been made. Judge Grey had also personally gone shopping, and had caused a number of parcels to be delivered to the hotel suite. New clothing for all, as well as trunks.

Now Judge Grey looked at Gideon squarely. "It's your decision, Mr. Mapes. It would probably be safe for you and your wife to stay here, or near here, until your leg heals further. Or I can remove you today, some distance from the river."

"I can stand any amount of pain to put space between us and the slave catchers," Gideon said grimly. "There was one on the boat, and only by chance that we found out."

This was news to Judge Grey. He looked at Roxana. "I'll tell you later," she said hastily, avoiding his eyes.

"Then I'll see about making arrangements for us to leave tonight," the judge said, and left. He did not tell them where they would be going, and no one asked.

"I'm going out, too," Roxana said abruptly a short while later. Joss offered to go along, but Roxana shook her head quickly. This was one errand she needed to do alone.

She put on one of the outfits her father had selected—he'd been a good judge of size, and the skirts came demurely to her ankles—did up her hair, put on the new broad-brimmed straw hat. Then she went down to the front desk and asked if there was a list of the survivors. Only of those who could identify themselves, she was told; nothing of those too severely hurt to speak, and only limited identity of the dead. The one good thing was that the list of identified survivors included those still across the river. The desk clerk pointed to where it was posted by the door.   .

Roxana was just crossing towards it when a tearful voice called, "Miss Darden . . . oh, Miss Darden . . ."

Miss Hannaford was sitting in an armchair, looking small and lost in a borrowed dress that was much too large. Roxana went to her, and the older woman held out her hands. "Oh, my dear, I'm so glad you're all right . . . but whatever shall we do?"

Roxana glanced around and felt an inner chill. "Mrs. Raeburn?" she asked gently.

Miss Hannaford shook her head. "Whatever shall I do?" she murmured like a bewildered child. "Sister's always looked after everything, and now she's gone . . ."

"Don't worry. My—my uncle will take care of things here for you, and see you get safely home." Roxana felt cruel leaving the old woman, but there was something that she had to do.

She went to the posted lists. There was no Carlton Tanner listed among the living or the dead. She returned to the desk and asked about what the desk clerk delicately called "the remains." They were all in the ballroom now, united in death regardless of race or class. The injured had either left or been distributed to hotels and families around the city.

What shocked her most, once she'd steeled herself to enter the ballroom, was the *orderliness* of the scene. The floor had been covered with newspapers, and the bodies laid out in orderly rows. Men on one side, women on the other . . . separated by sex, even though no longer by race or class, in some hideous parody of morality. They were covered, wholly or partially, by whatever shrouds the rescuers could provide . . . tablecloths, yard goods, curtains, sheets. There was no one to assist her. She had to make her way, as a few other survivors or curious were doing, from one body to another.

By the time she had viewed the first dozen faces anguished or serene in death, she no longer gagged.

It was some half hour and many bodies later that she found him. His face was peaceful, despite the crushing wound where ship's debris must have struck his head with considerable force.

"Friend? Or family member?" inquired the guard she summoned. He looked as though he hadn't slept, and he held a small notepad and pencil.

"An acquaintance. His name is Carlton Tanner, and he's from somewhere south." That was probably not his real name, but it was as good a one as any. He had been charming, he had been amusing. He had awakened in her feelings for which she had not been prepared. And he'd died because he had gone back for Joss. Not because he cared what happened to her; to him she was a piece of property. He'd done it for Roxana. To please her? To impress her? She'd never know, and it made no difference.

She went back to the hotel lobby, where she met up with her father and introduced him—as her uncle—to Miss Hannaford. Judge Grey "took care of things" for the old lady, as she'd known he would, even down to delicately loaning money. They managed to get away without giving her their home address.

Dusk was falling before Joss and Gideon were put into a wagon and driven away—to where, Roxana did not know, and because of onlookers she dared not ask. Soon afterward, she, the judge, and Golden Lad left also, in a carriage with the judge at the reins. "Why couldn't we have gone with—" Roxana started to say, and the judge motioned her to silence.

To her surprise they drove to the next town and left the carriage at a livery stable. Then, guided by her father,

they walked a mile through the countryside. Even Golden
Lad, for a change, was silent. "This way," Judge Grey said
finally. He held some low-hanging branches to one side,
and Roxana ducked under them. Then she gasped.

There stood the wagon with Joss and Gideon, with nobody at the reins.

Golden Lad jumped up quickly and curled himself next
to Gideon. Judge Grey lifted Roxana to the seat and swung
himself up beside her; picked up the reins and clucked to
the horse, which moved off docilely. They rolled into
deeper country without speaking. A strange sort of calm
seemed to have settled on Roxana—half acceptance, half
plain weariness. At last the wagon stopped before a pleasant, dark-stained house set amid spreading fields. No lamps
burned, but the judge went to the door, unlocked it, and
came back to speak to Joss. "Can you help me bring your
husband in?"

Joss nodded. Together they leveraged Gideon, his teeth
gritted in pain, onto his one good leg and supported him
as he hopped to the house. "There's a table with a lamp
and matches straight ahead," Judge Grey told Joss.

Soon lamplight flickered on a spacious kitchen. Its shutters were closed, and at the judge's direction Roxana carried
the lamp across the hall and lit the lamps in the simple
parlor.

"Who lives here?" she asked, returning to the kitchen.

"We do, for a few weeks, if you're willing." The judge
turned to Joss. "If you'll do the cooking and nursing, you
can stay here until the leg knits more. Otherwise, I can
arrange for you to be transported to the next station in the
morning, and Roxana and I will go back home."

"The longer the time before Gideon travels on that leg,
the better," Joss said firmly.

So it was decided. There were two bedrooms upstairs, as well as a downstairs one for Gideon and Joss. Roxana found sheets and pillowcases and made up the beds while Joss and her father settled Gideon for the night. She peeped in the cupboards and found an ample food supply—even butter, milk, and meat in an icebox. And peanuts; Joss could make Mam Lucy's famous "medicinal" peanut soup.

"Whose house is this?" she asked her father on their way upstairs, and he answered only, "It belongs to a relative of a client."

But you just happen to have the keys, Roxana added mentally. She didn't ask further. It was an Underground Railroad station, and the less knowledge shared, the better.

She awoke early the next morning to a world filled with sunshine. Beyond the low window of her little room spread rolling fields, golden in the summer sun. Somewhere close at hand a bird was singing. Far off on a hillside she saw the small figures of a man and a dog. *Papa and Golden Lad . . .*

Roxana dressed quickly and hurried after them. Golden Lad heard and ran to meet her, leaping with delight. Her father waited, smiling.

"Pretty day, isn't it?" he asked.

Roxana took a deep breath. "Yes, it is."

For the first time in a long while . . . for the first time ever, maybe . . . she was filled with a sense of peace . . . and promise.

They walked further up the hill without speaking, found a low stone wall, and sat down on it companionably. Roxana found a stick and threw it for Golden Lad. He raced downhill after it, his plumed tail rampant.

"That dog's grown so much," Judge Grey commented.

Roxana didn't answer, and the words hung in the air, gathering a wider meaning.

"I have to tell you something," she said abruptly. And did, all about Carlton Tanner.

"You have nothing for which to blame yourself—in any sense," Judge Grey said. "All we can ever do is the best we can, according to whatever light the good Lord gives us."

"That's what Miss Hattie says, too."

"You did what you felt you had to do."

Roxana wasn't sure to what, specifically, her father was referring. Perhaps all of it, she concluded. "I'm very proud of you," the judge went on. "Especially of your going on the river."

"As you said, it's what we had to do." Roxana swung round to face her father, hugging her knees. "What now, Papa?"

To her surprise, Judge Grey paused for several minutes before replying. "As I said earlier, that depends on you. We can go home today, or we can stay till Joss and Gideon leave—"

"We stay."

"—after which, we'll go back to Grey's Landing for the rest of August. After that . . . I told you on your birthday I was needed in Washington on urgent business. Some of it to do with slavery and the slave catchers, but not all. This has been a turbulent year for our country, Roxana, and next year looks to be one also, in many fields. We'll have a national election in November, and President Jackson will go out of office next March. He will, I think, be succeeded by Vice President Van Buren, a New Yorker and an Anti-Slavery proponent."

Judge Grey paused again and Roxana waited. *He's talking about politics to me*, she realized, astonished. *About his work.* A lot *had* changed.

"As you may know, I've been asked to run for office in

the past," Judge Grey went on. "At first the timing wasn't right, or I felt I could do more good behind the scenes. I did consider running two years ago. . . ."

He didn't go on; he didn't need to. Two years ago this past May, her mother and her brother had died.

"I couldn't leave Grey's Landing then," her father said. "But now . . . so much has changed. Particularly now that Joss will be gone. It will be very lonely at Grey's Landing for you without her. Would you want to go back to Miss Beecher's school, Roxana? You can if you want to. Or, if I were elected to office, you could go with me. Not as my official hostess, in the political sense," he added, chuckling. "You're a bit too young yet for that. But on an everyday basis, you could run our home. Mam Lucy's too old, and too settled in at Grey's Landing, to be uprooted. We might take Caesar, though."

"I couldn't go back to Miss Beecher's school, even if I wanted to," Roxana said. "It's all but closed. Miss Hattie's married, and practically a mother, and Miss Catherine's off somewhere. I'd rather be with you." She looked at her father, her eyes twinkling. "Even though it will mean ankle-length skirts, and pinned-up hair, and corsets!"

"I'm quite sure your mother would say it's time for those things anyway," her father retorted. "I definitely remember her being quite the young lady when she was fourteen!"

They both laughed. *Like Miss Hattie promised, the pain does go away . . . for both of us.*

"It wouldn't necessarily be Washington," her father cautioned. "Elections are always uncertain. That's why I personally would prefer an appointment—to the federal government, or to Indiana's, which is also a possibility. There's even been talk of a ministerial appointment for me to England, if Mr. Van Buren's elected. But that would mean traveling on the ocean."

Roxana took a deep breath and gazed across the ripening fields, at the brilliant sky and at Golden Lad, joyfully plunging up the hill. How could she reassure her father, make him understand how much had changed?

"I've crossed over Jordan, Papa," she said.

Author's Notes

(Adapted from Author's Note in *Harriet: The Life and World of Harriet Beecher Stowe* by Norma Johnston, copyright © 1994 by Dryden Harris St. John, Inc.)

About Race and Language in this Book:

What is correct or incorrect in spelling, grammar, punctuation, and connotations of words is continually evolving. Many words used at the time the events in *Over Jordan* took place have no meaning to us at all. Many then commonly used are nowadays shocking. What is "proper" (in language and behavior) is constantly changing.

Nowhere is this as true as in the language of race. Wherever possible, in *Over Jordan*, I have referred to the two races represented in the story in what linguistically are parallel terms—*white* and *black*. There are a few times, however, when using the word "Negro" or insulting variations of it has been unavoidable—on the poster advertising for the return of runaway slaves, and in the language spoken by the slave catchers. Actually, in the nineteenth century the "proper" (polite) term for persons of African descent was not black (which they would have found offensive) but Negro. The word (from the Latin *niger*, meaning "black") has been so debased by derogatory use that it is no longer acceptable at the end of the twentieth century and beyond. It took the American slave trade to debase the word . . . It took a war (spurred on by a book; see below) to eliminate slavery in America . . . It took the civil rights movement to make the word *black* synonymous with *proud*.

About Harriet Beecher Stowe and her Family:

Every once in a while a book appears that shakes the world. *Uncle Tom's Cabin*, a story of slavery and the Underground Railway, in large part told from the perspective of the slaves themselves, was one of those books. It caused a firestorm of controversy in this country and abroad, forced complacent whites to come face-to-face with slavery's horrors, and ultimately led to Abraham Lincoln's telling the author that she was "the little woman who wrote the book that made this great war" and brought about the thirteenth amendment to the U.S. Constitution, which abolished slavery forever.

That small, shy housewife was Harriet Beecher Stowe, Roxana Grey's beloved "Miss Hattie" in *Over Jordan*. And she was no ordinary housewife. A descendant of the Puritans, a teacher when she was only fourteen, she was the daughter, wife, sister, and mother of preachers. She was also a born storyteller. It is difficult for us today to realize the enormity of the Beecher family's fame. In a time before radio, movies, or TV, authors were major celebrities, and preachers who toured the nation's pulpits and lecture platforms were superstars. The Beechers were the greatest of the great. Lyman Beecher and his dazzling son Henry Ward Beecher were national celebrities, national role models, national icons. Harriet Beecher Stowe was the first American superstar author, and to her astonishment (and probably her brothers' chagrin) eclipsed them all. Her fame has outlasted that of all her kin.

About the Underground Railway:
Many men and women, young and old, risked their lives to flee from slavery with no map other than to "follow the drinking gourd" (the Big Dipper in the night sky, in which the North Star pointed the way to freedom in the north). Many others, both black and white, also risked life and liberty to help them. Their network of secret routes and hiding places came to be known as the Underground Railway. To learn more about it, ask your town or school librarian. Some of the most famous Railway "conductors," all former slaves, were Harriet Tubman, Sojourner Truth, and Frederick Douglass; many biographies have been written about them. Norma Johnston's biography of Harriet Beecher Stowe, *Harriet: The Life and World of Harriet Beecher Stowe*, is published by Beech Tree Books/William Morrow and Company.

RECIPES MENTIONED IN
OVER JORDAN

+ Chicken with Oranges and Pecans +

2 ½ to 3 pounds chicken pieces; split chicken breasts
  and/or thighs (bones-in or boneless)
1 cup cooking oil
1 tablespoon paprika
1 teaspoon dried thyme leaves
1 teaspoon dried oregano leaves
½ teaspoon ground coriander
¼ teaspoon coarse-ground black pepper
¼ teaspoon coarse-ground (kosher) salt
1 medium onion, cut in half lengthwise and then thinly sliced
1 large can mandarin orange segments, drained
½ cup shelled pecans
¾ cup orange juice

Pull off and discard as much skin and fat from chicken
pieces as possible. Set chicken pieces aside. In a large bowl,

combine next 7 ingredients. Dip *half* the chicken pieces into mixture in bowl, then spread them across bottom of 4-quart casserole or heavy roasting pan. Scatter *half* the sliced onions over top. Repeat with remaining chicken and onions. Pour remaining contents of bowl over chicken in casserole. Cover with lid. Bake in 375° oven for 45 minutes. Add orange segments, pecans, and orange juice to contents of casserole and stir in. Continue baking for 15 to 30 minutes, or until top pieces of chicken are tender when pierced with a fork.

Approximately 1 large or 2 small pieces per serving

To freeze leftover chicken: Wrap individual pieces tightly in foil, or place 2 to 4 pieces together in freezer containers, and freeze.

✦ Mam Lucy's Rice Pilaf ✦

1 cup regular long-grain rice or 2 cups instant rice
1 cup orzo
1 teaspoon paprika
½ teaspoon dried thyme leaves
½ teaspoon ground coriander
¼ teaspoon salt*
⅛ teaspoon coarse-ground pepper
3 cups chicken broth or 1½ cups each water and orange juice
½ cup slivered almonds (optional)
*If chicken broth is salty, do *not* add salt.

In 2-quart casserole, combine all ingredients except chicken broth and almonds. Bring chicken broth to boil and add to casserole. Stir well and cover. Bake in 350° to 400° oven for 20 minutes. Stir rice, adding almonds if desired. If it's too dry, add ¼ to ½ cup liquid (chicken broth, orange juice, or water). If rice is not fully cooked, return to oven for another 10 to 15 minutes.

Approximately 8 servings

To freeze leftover rice: Spread rice out flat in zip-top plastic freezer bags. Freeze *flat*. To serve, break off the quantity of rice needed, transfer to ovenproof/microwaveable casserole, cover, and heat in oven or microwave.

✦ Groundnut (Peanut) Soup ✦

1 medium onion, finely chopped
2 ribs celery, finely chopped
4 tablespoons butter
3 tablespoons flour
1 cup smooth peanut butter
4 cups chicken broth
4 cups milk or half-and-half
6 teaspoons chopped peanuts
cracked red pepper (optional)

In a saucepan (or casserole that can be used on stovetop), melt butter over low heat and sauté onion and celery until soft and translucent but not brown. Stir in flour until well blended. Add peanut butter and cook, stirring constantly, until peanut butter begins to soften. Add chicken broth, a little at a time, stirring constantly until peanut butter is thoroughly blended with the liquid. Bring to a boil, then remove from heat and blend in milk or half-and-half. Return to low heat for a few minutes, but do not allow to come to a boil. (Soup can be removed from heat and refrigerated at this point, and then reheated when needed. Do not let it boil!) Serve at once, garnished with chopped peanuts. Pass the cracked red pepper for those who want to make the soup "hotter."

Approximately 6 to 8 servings

J
F
JOH

Johnston, Norma

Over Jordan

$15.00